THE KELLYHORNS

Which was Pam and which was Penny?

THE KELLYHORNS

Barbara Cooney

HYPERION
NEW YORK

 For information address Volo Books, 114 Fifth Avenue, New York, New York 10011-5690.

First Volo edition, 2001
1 3 5 7 9 10 8 6 4 2

The text for this book is set in 13-point Deepdene.

Library of Congress Cataloging-in-Publication Data
Cooney, Barbara, 1917–
The Kellyhorns / by Barbara Cooney.—1st Volo ed.
p. cm.
Summary: Pam and Penny Kellyhorn are eleven-year-old twins, one living with an aunt, the other with their father and cousin, in small towns in Maine and have just met, but it doesn't take them long to learn to be sisters as together they help bring an arsonist to justice, and try to rekindle the romance between Aunt Ivory and Puppa.
ISBN 0-7868-1522-1 — ISBN 0-7868-1523-X
[1. Twins—Fiction. 2. Sisters—Fiction. 3. Family life—Maine—Fiction. 4. Circus performers—Fiction. 5. Maine—Fiction.] I. Title.
PZ7.C783 Ke 2001
[Fic]—dc21 00-63388

Visit www.volobooks.com

To my twin

CONTENTS

PART I
AUTUMN

CHAPTER ONE

October 4-5-6

NOW DON'T DO anything dangerous," Aunt Ivory admonished Pamela. She gave her a fifty-cent piece. "You have to buy your lunch out of that, so don't spend it all at once." Pamela was inching toward the door. "And don't get your dress dirty," Aunt Ivory called. "Remember you're a young lady!"

Today was October 4th. All summer long a banner had hung across Twidboro's Main Street—from a nail above Bud's Barbershop to one above Preble's Shoe Store—and it bore the message UXTON FAIR, OCTOBER 4-5-6. And today was October 4th. Every winter Aunt Ivory made a patchwork quilt, and every fall she exhibited it at the Uxton Fair and won first prize. Even when they had lived back country, they had gone to the Uxton Fair. The world would have come to an end if Aunt Ivory had failed to return home with the blue ribbon. That was the high spot of the year for Aunt Ivory. So today was her day. And Pamela didn't have to go to school. They had got up early and taken the bus to Uxton. It was still early, but Aunt Ivory wanted to be in the exhibition hall while the judging was going on. For once she had no time to be bothered with Pamela. So Aunt Ivory had sent Pamela off with a fifty-cent piece while she herself stayed with trembling knees amid the quilts and hooked rugs and preserves and squashes in the exhibition hall. Pamela trotted off eagerly with her two brown pigtails bouncing on her back and her brown eyes shining shyly from beneath the brim of the hat that Aunt Ivory made her wear. She was dressed very tidily in a dark blue dress that was longer than the dresses of any of the other girls she knew. It was Aunt Ivory's idea.

"You're twelve years old now," she had said on Pamela's birthday. "It's time you let down the hems of your dresses." So Pamela had spent her twelfth birthday letting down the hems of her dresses. She had one of these on today. She also wore long socks. Dark blue, too. For a brief moment Pamela wished she looked more like the other girls she saw on the fairground.

But then she forgot about it, because there were to be oxen pulls that morning. She went across the fairground to the enclosure where the farmers were competing to see who owned the strongest pair of oxen. Already they had started. Men in freshly laundered blue denim suits and their womenfolk and children leaned against the fence of the enclosure watching intently. Sometimes they talked among themselves, wagering on whose team would win. Now and then they shouted words of encouragement. Pamela hurried over to them. A dirty pair of black-and-white oxen were now trying to haul the stoneboat loaded with granite blocks to one end of the enclosure. They leaned forward, their necks straining, their muscles bulging, and their knobby legs pushing back against the earth. When they reached the end, their sandy-haired owner turned them around by jabbing at them with a nail-tipped stick. Slowly, painfully, zigzagging their load, they got halfway back across the pen. And then they could go no farther. It was a cruel sight. The owner's face got red, and he jabbed harder than ever with his stick. But the poor patient oxen could do no more. Pamela shuddered as she watched the unfeeling Rusty Hanna angrily prodding them until they bled. She had hoped that he would not show up this year. She had watched the same terrifying procedure last year. That was the time when she had seen Hiram Crimmins capture the red ribbon with his new yoke of Jersey oxen. This year, though, they were older, and Hiram hoped he would be able to take home a blue ribbon to pin up beside the red one over the feed bin in his barn. Pamela was hoping so too. For Hiram Crimmins was a new friend of hers. She and Aunt Ivory had lived back country until last summer. Then Aunt Ivory had had to sell the house and they had returned to the old family manse in Twidboro. That was where Hiram Crimmins lived. And Pamela and Hiram had struck up a friendship. She looked around for him. And then she saw his yoke of white-faced oxen. The brass tips on their curved horns shone in the sun, and the sides of their brown bellies gleamed with currying. Pamela left her place at the fence and went over to them. Hiram stood beside his oxen absentmindedly stroking the nearest one's rump as he watched the purple-faced Rusty Hanna lead his pair out of the enclosure.

"Hi, Pam," Hiram called, catching sight of her.

"Hi, Hiram," said Pamela shyly. Then she added, "I came."

"I see you did. I guess I'll have to get the

blue ribbon then. I can't let you go home disappointed."

There were four more pairs to go before Hiram's.

"That pair there," said Hiram, pointing to a white pair just entering the enclosure, "that pair there is mighty strong. We sure will have to go some to beat them." And he was right. It was the same pair that had taken first prize the year before. This year they dragged the stoneboat even farther.

"Whew!" whistled Hiram. He got out his red handkerchief and wiped his face. "We sure will have to be good."

Finally it was Hiram's turn. He clucked his tongue to Star and Bright and they followed him out into the ring. Pamela held her breath with the crowd as slowly, slowly Star and Bright pulled the heavy granite blocks across the enclosure. Slowly they zigzagged the load until they had passed Rusty Hanna's mark.

"Nary a stick," said one man near Pamela

reverently. For though Hiram Crimmins carried a stick, he never used it. He clucked his tongue and used soft words, but he never used the stick.

"He can't make it," said the man, as Star and Bright, with every muscle bulging, neared the mark of the white oxen. Inch by inch the stoneboat moved. But so slowly that Pamela thought only a miracle could make it pass the mark. And then the crowd let out its breath. A wave of clapping fluttered around the fence. Hiram Crimmins had passed the mark! Pamela ducked out while the men congratulated Hiram. It was all man-talk now. What kind of grain did he use? and who was the sire? and who the dam?

So Pamela trotted back to the amusement area. It was dinnertime now. She looked at the signs. HAMBURGERS 5¢, HOT DOGS 5¢, OYSTER STEW 15¢, SANDWICHES, COFFEE, SOFT DRINKS, POPCORN. She decided on two hot dogs and a glass of milk—which left her thirty cents. Ten of these she invested in a game of Beano in hopes of winning a white fur cat for Aunt Ivory. But she did not win.

Now what'll I do? Pamela asked herself. Toss pennies? Two sailors were leaning over the rail rapidly losing their pennies. Or shall I play one of the ring games? Or bet on the Wheel of Chance and be the lucky winner of an Indian blanket? Or knock the wooden milk bottles over and win an orange plaster dog with silver sprinkled on him? Pamela wandered around trying to make up her mind. If only Aunt Ivory hadn't said not to do anything dangerous. Well, the merry-go-round wasn't dangerous. Certainly not.

I'll go on that. It's got awfully pretty horses, Pamela told herself. But she eyed the Tilt-A-Whirl enviously. And the Ferris wheel. She scuffed slowly past the Tilt-A-Whirl.

"Room for one more!" cried the barker. "Spin till you scream! The most thrilling ride on the grounds! How about you, young lady?" he called to Pamela. She stopped scuffing. And her face grew red. She was sure that everyone was looking at her.

"Come on!" someone called. "We need one more. It's fun!" Pamela looked up into the eyes of a girl just about her own age sitting in one of the cars of the Tilt-A-Whirl. "Come on," she urged again. She looked very nice and friendly and the little boy sitting beside her did too. Pamela forgot all about Aunt Ivory's warning.

"That's it, miss. One dime," said the barker, as Pamela handed over one of her dimes. "That car over there." He pointed to the one in which the girl and the little boy were sitting. Pamela climbed in beside them.

"You don't slide around so much with three," said the little boy. And they were off. The Tilt-A-Whirl went around in a circle like a merry-go-round, but it went up and down in waves at the same time and the little cars spun around in circles all the while—sometimes slowly and sometimes so fast it made the riders scream.

"Christmas!" shouted the little boy. "It's wonderful!"

"I'll say!" cried the girl. Pamela thought so too. She had never done anything like it before in her life. The ride ended long before they wanted it to.

"Do you want to go on it again?" the girl asked Pamela.

"I have only one dime left," Pamela said.

"Have you been on the Ferris wheel yet?" asked the little boy.

Pamela shook her head.

"Oh, you've got to go," said the girl. "We are planning to go and if you want to spend your last dime that way, why, we'd love to have you come with us."

"I'd like that," said Pamela.

"What's your name?" they asked each other on the way over to the Ferris wheel. And so Pamela found out that the girl was called Penny and the boy was Barney "who isn't exactly my brother, but practically," Penny explained. The three of them got into one car as the two sailors got out. And up they went high above the fair.

They could see the whole grounds. The enclosure where horses had taken the place of oxen in the weight-pulling contests, the building where the livestock was stabled, and the poultry exhibit to the left. And down below, the Pitch-Till-U Win games, and Beano, and the shooting galleries, and men trying to drive nails into a piece of two-by-four with one blow. The merry-go-round, and the Strange As It Seems tent, and the Athletic Arena, where a hairy man in green tights was challenging anyone in the crowd to come up and wrestle with him.

"Puppa beat him last year," said Penny proudly, pointing to the hairy wrestler. "Boy! It was scary."

Pamela's eyes were wide in admiration of her newfound friend. She looked down again at the fairground. Over to the right was the Home Products Exhibit with its prize cakes and fruit and vegetables and 4-H Club displays. Mammoth yellow squashes and orange pumpkins, fodder beets and great polished apples.

And the preserves and rugs and quilts of the ladies of the county.

"My goodness," Pamela cried. "The quilt! Aunt Ivory!"

"What's wrong?" asked Penny.

"My aunt Ivory," said Pamela. "She told me not to do anything dangerous."

"Dangerous!" exclaimed Penny. "This isn't dangerous. Look. You can rock it as hard as you want and nothing happens." Penny and Barney commenced rocking the seat. The Ferris wheel had stopped turning, and they hung high above the fairground as someone got out below and a new customer got in.

"See," they said, "nothing happens." And nothing did. It was scary and exciting but nothing happened. Pamela commenced rocking with them.

"If you want to go on something scary, you ought to go on the roller coaster at Old Orchard," Barney informed her as they went rocking around the circle. And around they went while Barney and Penny recounted their adventures at Old Orchard. Rocking all the time.

"You know," Barney said, "you and Penny look an awful lot alike. If you took off your hat and didn't have bangs and wore overalls, I bet you'd look just like her. Go ahead," he said, "take it off. Let's see."

"Don't do it if you don't want to, Pamela," said Penny. "You look so nice and neat with it on. The trouble with Barney is that he is always thinking he has found my long-lost twin. I have one, you know," she went on. "But after Mumma died when we were born, some relative came and took her away. There was a fight or something. So I've never seen her. I know she lives in Maine somewhere. But nobody ever talks about her. Just Barney. He's always looking for her."

"Well," said Pamela, joking, "maybe I'm her. Besides I'm tired of looking neat." She pulled off her hat.

"Push back your bangs a minute," said Barney. Pamela pushed them back.

"Boy!" cried Barney. "We've found her! It's the twin!"

The engine of the Ferris wheel stopped. "Your ride is up," said the attendant, and they got out. Pamela was staring at Penny. Except for the overalls and the bangs and a few freckles it was like looking in the mirror. Penny was staring at Pamela.

"Maybe," she said, "you really are."

"Pamela Kellyhorn!" It was Aunt Ivory. "Come here this instant. I thought I told you not to do anything dangerous. Where's your hat? You look a fright." Aunt Ivory took Pamela by the hand and led her away.

"But, Aunt Ivory . . ." But there was no such word as "but" for Aunt Ivory, and before she could say another word to Penny and Barney, Pamela was well on her way to the fairground exit. Looking back she could see them talking excitedly together, and then they were lost to sight. Aunt Ivory scolded her all the way to the bus stop. But when they got into the bus she just sat looking out of the window and didn't say a word. She didn't even mention the quilt.

"Hiram Crimmins got first with his oxen," Pamela ventured.

"That's nice," said Aunt Ivory. She looked tired and her mouth drooped. Maybe if the quilt were mentioned they might have a more cheerful ride home.

"What about the quilt?" Pamela asked.

Aunt Ivory didn't say anything. She merely snapped open her big, black pocketbook and pulled out a red ribbon. It explained now why Aunt Ivory had been so unusually cross about the Ferris wheel. As far as she knew, Aunt Ivory had never won anything less than first prize with her quilts before.

CHAPTER TWO

Aunt Ivory's Past

IMOGENE AND PAMELA sat on an old log that had been washed up on the shore of Alewife River. The Alewife was a tidal river—more an inlet of the ocean than a river. Up above the town of Twidboro were the falls where the fresh water met the salt. In the spring the alewives swam up the salt river and leaped up the falls to spawn in the fresh water. And so the river had been called Alewife River. Pamela and Imogene sat on the edge of it now. It was Saturday, a chilly blue day about a week after the fair. That morning, when Pamela was doing the dishes, a knock came on the door. The person didn't wait but came in just as Aunt Ivory said, "Come in."

"Why, hello, Imogene," she said. Imogene Elliott was two years older than Pamela. Aunt Ivory thought Imogene was nice. And she was. To Aunt Ivory. She was polite and helpful and always jumping up to do things. Almost too helpful, thought Pamela. But she never said so. She knew that at home Imogene pretended not to hear when her mother asked her to do something. She only helped if she couldn't get out of it. She knew, too, that Imogene talked back to her mother, and that the reason no one else knew about it was that her mother was too proud to admit that she had a lazy, rude daughter. Aunt Ivory, for instance, thought Imogene a paragon of virtue and was always glad to see her, and she was more than pleased when Imogene, who was fourteen, deigned to play with Pamela, who was twelve. But Pamela knew it was because she had no other friends.

"I came to ask Pam to come take a walk with me," Imogene simpered.

Aunt Ivory beamed. Imogene was such a

nice, ladylike friend for Pamela. "Here, I'll finish the dishes, Pamela," said Aunt Ivory. "You can run along."

"But I promised Nancy I'd come over this morning. We were going to—"

Aunt Ivory interrupted and said why couldn't Nancy come along. But that would never have done. Pamela couldn't say that Nancy didn't like Imogene.

"Yes," said Imogene. "Let's get Nancy."

"No, never mind," said Pamela. She hated being along when Imogene and Nancy were together, because the air was always electric with Nancy's displeasure. Nancy never made any bones about her feelings. She never pretended to be something she wasn't, the way Imogene did. Imogene never noticed anything, though. She was too thick-skinned.

"Nancy has to help her mother for a while anyhow," Pamela said.

"Well, run along, children," said Aunt Ivory. "And, Pamela, get your heavy sweater.

It's chilly outside, isn't it, Imogene?"

"Yes," said Imogene, "*real* cold today, Miss Perry," in her sweetest voice.

It *was* coolish out of the sun but warm in it, and they really did not need their sweaters. The air was clear and crisp, and wood smoke drifted from all the chimneys on Elm Street into the bright blue sky. Pamela was thinking how nice it had been of Aunt Ivory to finish the dishes.

Now they were down on the shore, and Pamela had just emerged from one of her last swims of the season. Aunt Ivory would not have approved of her swimming so late in the year. Nor would she have approved of swimming without a bathing suit. Pamela wondered whether Imogene would tell. The water had been cold. Icy cold. Though not as cold as downriver in the ocean, because when the tide went out, the mud flats were heated by the sun and that helped take the chill off the water. Imogene had not gone swimming. Because the water was too cold and not because her mother wouldn't let her, as she had said. Her mother didn't allow her to use nail polish, either, but nevertheless all ten of her toes were painted scarlet when she took off her shoes and socks to test the water. Pamela sat in the sun drying the ends of her pigtails. The breasts of a flock of snipes flying close to the water flashed white in the sun as they wheeled and flew across the river. Imogene was complaining because the polish on her left big toenail was peeling. Pamela wished Nancy had come. She and Nancy were vying with each other for the honor of being the first one to go swimming in the spring and the last one to go swimming this fall. But things like that didn't interest Imogene.

"Your aunt Ivory is a queer duck," said Imogene, as she examined her toes. The fur stood up on Pamela's back. Nobody could say anything against Aunt Ivory. Aunt Ivory, it was true, was always admonishing her not to do this and not to do that and to wear her rubbers and act like a lady, but strict as she was, she was genuinely fond of Pamela and Pamela of her. Besides, she was the only excuse for a mother that Pamela had. And, as she sometimes had to tell herself when Aunt Ivory was being over-strict, it was all for her own good. Deep down inside, Pamela felt sorry for Aunt Ivory because she never seemed to have any fun. None except her cats and the annual quilt. Now even the quilt had failed her. At thirty-three she had a lonely, uninteresting life, and the villagers thought her odd. But they accepted her as she was. The more old-maidish she became, the more the Twidboro people indulged her. For wasn't she the daughter of Joseph Kellyhorn, who had been the well-beloved minister of the Twidboro Congregational Church until his death twelve years ago? And if Aunt Ivory scolded the man at the store for trying to give her a bad grade of cat food when her cats used only the best, he would only smile and redouble his efforts to please her. There seemed to be an unwritten agreement among the villagers to be as nice as they could to Aunt Ivory. Sometimes it puzzled Pamela that people were so indulgent with her. Once last summer she heard Nancy's grandfather, Gramp Drake, say, "Aw, Ivory Perry, she don't mean nawthin'. It's jest her way. She ain't had an easy life. Mebbe she never starved or nawthin', but still—" Pamela was dying to ask him what he meant. But she didn't dare. Except with Nancy, she was shy with the Twidboro people still. Not with Imogene, of course, but then Imogene didn't count.

"I said," repeated Imogene, "your aunt Ivory is a queer duck."

"I heard you the first time," Pamela said. "And I don't think you have any right to say that."

"Well, she is," Imogene insisted.

"She's always nice to you," Pamela said as evenly as she could.

"Oh, I know how to get along with old ladies all right," Imogene said loftily.

"Well, she wouldn't like you so much if she

could see that red stuff on your toenails." Pamela was getting angry. After all, Aunt Ivory might be old-fashioned and strict, but that didn't give Imogene the right to call her a "queer duck." And she wasn't an old lady yet either.

"You don't need to get so nasty about it," said Imogene. "I was just going to tell you something about her. About why she's so queer."

Pamela didn't say anything. If she wanted to know anything about her aunt Ivory's past she didn't want to hear it from Imogene.

"Aren't you interested?" asked Imogene. She was piqued by Pamela's apparent lack of interest.

"No," said Pamela.

"You will be when you hear," said Imogene importantly, as she gave up gazing at her feet and began to put on her shoes and stockings. "The reason," she said slowly, and she charged each word with meaning, "the reason your Aunt Ivory isn't quite right in her upper story *is that she was disappointed in love*. Put that in your smoke and pipe it," she added facetiously; and without waiting for Pamela, turned and started to scramble up the bank. "I've got to get home to lunch. Hang these blackberry bushes, anyhow. I always end up a bloody pulp when I take a walk with you, Pamela Kellyhorn."

Pamela thoughtfully put on her clothes. The trouble with Imogene Elliott, she told herself, was that she read too many of these love and romance magazines. Her bottom drawer was filled with them.

That night after supper when the dishes were done, Aunt Ivory sat in the kitchen rocker doing nothing but stroking the white cat that lay in her lap and vaguely listening to a mixture of static and music on the radio. Ever since the quilt episode she hadn't been her old busy self. It worried Pamela. In former years, as soon as the fair was over, out would come the ragbag, and Pamela and Aunt Ivory would sit down on the kitchen floor and pore over the rags, picking out the prettiest pieces for next fall's quilt. But this time the ragbag remained hanging on its nail in the attic. Aunt Ivory had said, "Some other time," to Pamela when twice she had offered to go get the ragbag.

"How about a game of double solitaire, Aunt Ivory?" Pamela asked.

"Is your homework done?"

"Yes," said Pamela. "Besides, it's Sunday tomorrow."

"Well, all right, dear."

Pamela jumped up. Terms of endearment were rare on Aunt Ivory's lips.

"The cards are in the parlor, dear."

Dear, again! Pamela was in the parlor and back again almost before Aunt Ivory had finished speaking. They sat down at the kitchen table.

"Is it one up and six down or one up and seven down?" asked Aunt Ivory. "It's such a long time since I've played cards."

"One up and six down," said Pamela.

Aunt Ivory's hands were busy now and,

encouraged by the soft glow of the kerosene lamp on the red-checked tablecloth, she began to talk.

"You know," she said, "I used to play whist a lot when I was younger. Your mother and I used to play of a winter evening when we had callers. At this very table. There was one young man especially who liked to come and play with us. Three times a week regular he used to come."

"If you put that red eight on the black nine you'll have a space and then you can put your king in it," said Pamela. But she was listening hard. For the first time she was hearing about Aunt Ivory's past and about her mother, whom Aunt Ivory seldom mentioned.

"So I can," said Aunt Ivory, moving the red eight.

"I used to be a good double solitaire player too. We called it patience then," she continued. She laughed softly. "Sometimes Barnabas—that was the young man's name—and I would play patience together. But he always preferred whist. It was more exciting, I guess."

"Did he —was he in love with you?" Pamela was taken aback by her sudden boldness. With Aunt Ivory, of all people.

"I used to think so," said Aunt Ivory. And she sighed.

Pamela had just turned up the ace of spades, but she paused with it in midair, because Aunt Ivory had laid down her pack and softly folded her hands.

"As long as I've told you so much, Pamela, I might as well tell you the rest. Someone in Twidboro is bound to tell you sooner or later, anyhow.

"One morning, when I woke up, I looked over at your mother's bed. She and I used to sleep in the same room. Her bed hadn't been slept in. I couldn't understand it. The night before I had had a headache, so I had gone to bed leaving Kitty—that was your mother—hashing over the whist game with Barnabas. I quickly put on my clothes and went downstairs.

And there was our mother crying in Puppa's arms. Mumma had a note in her hand. She gave it to me. It said, 'Please forgive me. I have run off with Barnabas. We are going to get married. Please forgive me, Ivory, but we thought it would be easiest for you if we did it this way.' I was brokenhearted. But I didn't cry. I was furious. For you see, I loved Barnabas too. And Kitty knew it. That's why they ran off together. From that day on I wouldn't speak to either of them. I thought I hated them. Sometimes I still think I hate Barnabas for what he did to me. Then your mother died when you were born. And I took you and brought you up. I thought that somehow that would make up for the way I acted toward your mother."

"But didn't my father want me?" asked Pamela.

"Well, you see, dear, he couldn't bring up two babies by himself."

"Two babies!" cried Pamela. "Do I have a brother?"

"No," said Aunt Ivory. "You had a little twin sister."

"A twin sister! Oh, Aunt Ivory. Where is she? Tell me about her!"

"They may still live in Abbidydumkeag. I don't know. I've lost track of them. I never wanted to see Barnabas again. I should never have brought up the subject at all," said Aunt Ivory. "It's just—" She wiped her cheek. She couldn't be crying. Aunt Ivory never cried. "It's just that—well—" she said, "I know it's silly, but I guess I just feel badly about that quilt." She picked up her pack of cards. "Play your ace, Pamela, so that I can put on my two."

CHAPTER THREE

The Hen House

"PAM," SAID NANCY, "you've got to do something about it."

They were sitting out in the Hen House. It wasn't just a hen house; it was the Hen House. True, it was just a small gray shack sitting in the gooseberry patch behind Nancy's house. But it was more than that. It was the meeting place and refuge for Nancy's grandfather and his swarm of cronies. In the evenings they would gather there where they could talk like men and laugh loudly. In the kitchen with the women-folk, they were never at ease. They would keep their coats on and stretch their necks and pull at their collars and go home early. It wasn't the same thing at all as sitting on crates in the Hen

House with their pipes smoking and the stove's eyes shining through the grate. It wasn't the same thing at all as being boxed in, away from the feminine world, by the four small walls of the Hen House, which Gramp had decorated with the postcards he had collected since he was a boy. That was a long time ago so there were a great many postcards—postcards from Niagara Falls with silver sprinkled on the falls and postcards of the Floradora Sextet, six girls all alike in lavender dresses with ostrich feathers in their hats and black ribbons around their necks. There was one of a husky young woman in a pale blue, burly sweater and big bloomers with a football under one arm. "Nice legs," Gramp had once remarked to Nancy and Pam with a twinkle in his eye. But Nancy and Pam thought she was both funny and fat. And there were many others. They covered every bit of wall space. In the evenings a sign reading MEN ONLY hung on the outside of the door, but during the day Gramp would let Nancy and a few of her best friends use the Hen House. Gramp spent a lot of time there when he wasn't hauling wood. Even in the daytime. He was there with them now. The rain was drumming on the roof while the fire in the stove snapped warmly. Nancy and Pam had no secrets from Gramp.

"I'm just one of the girls," Gramp would say comfortably. And he would laugh a big laugh that rumbled up from his generous-sized stomach. They knew anything they said would never go farther than the door of the Hen House. Gramp knew how to keep a secret. He was in on this one too.

"Pam," Nancy continued, "you can't let your Aunt Ivory go on moping about her quilt."

"I don't think it's all the quilt," said Pam. "It's partly this Barnabas, only she never admitted it before." Pam found it hard to think of him as her father.

"Well, then we've got to find Barnabas. And your twin. I'll bet anything she's the same one you saw at the fair. Did you find out where she lived?"

Pam shook her head. "Besides," she said, "that one had a little brother."

"But she said he 'wasn't exactly a brother,' didn't she?"

"Yes." But Pam's face fell. "Maybe he's already married again. The little boy might be a junior. His name is Barney."

"Yes, and maybe he isn't married again. And the little boy's name might really be Bernard," said Nancy.

"But even if she is my twin, Aunt Ivory said she never wanted to set eyes on Barnabas again."

"Pamela Kellyhorn, do you or do you not want to find your twin and make your aunt Ivory happy all at the same time?"

"I do," said Pam. "It's only that it's all so important that I'm a little scared. Another thing, how are we going to find them? Aunt Ivory did say he used to live in Abbidydumkeag. How can we find out if he's still there?"

Gramp cleared his throat. "Is this Barnabas Kellyhorn we're talking about?" Gramp knew it was. He had been very attentive to the whole conversation though he was pretending he hadn't been.

"Yes. Pam's father. What do you think we ought to do, Gramp?" asked Nancy.

Gramp chewed on his pipe weighing the situation. "Ayah," he said, "I'd like to see Ivory Perry get hitched to Barnabas Kellyhorn." Gramp had known them both when they were young. Barnabas had had a hard time choosing between the pretty Perry girls. In the end he had chosen Kitty, Pam's mother. Now Ivory was getting to be more of an old maid every day, though she was still pretty and only thirty-three. It would be good for Ivory, he thought. And Pam, too. It wasn't easy on a girl to be brought up by a maiden aunt. Gramp chewed some more on his pipe. "Tell you what," he said, "next Saturday I've got to take a cord of wood down to Hatchet Cove, and I'll take you two along in the truck. It's only four miles farther to Abbidydumkeag. We can stop in and see if Barnabas still lives there."

Nancy jabbed Pam in the ribs with her elbow.

"Better not tell your aunt Ivory," said Gramp. "She wouldn't like if it she thought we were doing any matchmaking between her and Barnabas."

But Pam had no intention of telling.

"I'll just tell her we're going down to Hatchet Cove with you on business. That wouldn't be a lie."

"Okay," said Gramp. And he winked.

Saturday finally came. It was a clear, blue northwest day and puffs of white clouds ran before the wind. "This wind ought to be good for another three days," said Gramp. Nancy and Pam in big, thick sweaters were squashed under the gearshift of the old Ford truck. And Gramp wasn't any too thin either. They had started early and driven down the river road which followed the Alewife until it opened into the ocean at Hatchet Cove. The wind was ripping the last leaves off the trees, and they scuttled across the road in front of the truck. It was colder downriver at Hatchet Cove, and what leaves there were were yellow rather than red. The sea air, Gramp explained. For Hatchet Cove cut into the rim of Penobscot Bay.

Also on Penobscot Bay, and four miles farther out to sea on this arm of land, sat Abbidydumkeag. Gramp had deposited his cord of wood, and now they were on the last lap of the trip. The truck rattled into Abbidydumkeag. It was a little fishing village. The main street was nothing but a dirt road which ran along the brow of the crescent-shaped hill that cupped the harbor of Abbidydumkeag. Along the road were the homes of the fishermen and the lobstermen and the clam diggers. They were white clapboard houses for the most part, though some unpainted ones were a weather-beaten gray. And one beside the general store was almost black. In front of a house a seine was drying in the sun. The only other buildings along the road were the Grange Hall and a white wooden church with a steeple like a pile of children's blocks.

At the foot of the hill were the fish houses and the wharves. Stacks of lobster pots surrounded the fish houses. And pot buoys hung on their tattered gray sides. At each house the buoys were painted in different color combinations so that the owners could distinguish their own when they went to haul their traps. The wharves, too, were knee-deep in lobster pots and crowded with barrels and kegs and scales and derricks, for that was where the fishermen brought in their catches. Lobsters, flounders, haddock, hake, cod, mackerel. The wharves ran along the western half of the small deep harbor. Two lobster smacks were pulled up alongside the nearest one, and several more were moored out in the clear green water of the harbor with the other, smaller white-painted fishing boats.

At the mouth of the harbor sat an island crowned with spruce trees. A field of dry hay rolled down to the rocks on the south side—the sea side—of the island. Beyond the island, Penobscot Bay was blue and sparkling and dotted with white caps from the wind.

"Which is their house?" Pam asked.

Gramp pointed to the island. Near the top of the tan hill, visible around the corner of the spruce woods, with its back to the trees and its face to the sea was a house—a white, white house. Next to it, bright in the sun, was a white lighthouse.

"There. On Indian Island," said Gramp.

"Oh," cried Pam. And then she said, "Oh" again. Because it was almost too wonderful to be true.

"Come on," said Gramp. "We'll leave the car here by the store and see if we can find someone to row us out."

Pam and Nancy scrambled out of the truck. And they fell over one another in their hurry down the hill to the wharves, Gramp stepped into one of the buildings on the wharf at the bottom of the hill. The building reeked pungently of fish. The whole inside—the floors, the walls, the wide barrels, and even the men down at the farther end of the building—were covered with fish scales. Pam wrinkled her nose.

"You'll get used to it," said Gramp. In an undertone he added, "You'll have to if our plan works."

"Hi there, Sharm, you old codfish," called one of the men, catching sight of Gramp. Gramp's full name was Sherman Azariah Drake.

"Hi, Floyd," Gramp shouted. "Is Barnabas Kellyhorn still out on Indian?"

The men nodded.

"Thought mebbe I could find someone to row us out if he was."

"Sure thing," said Floyd. They followed him along the wharf and down the runway leading to the float. It was steep because the tide was going out.

"Here she is," said Floyd, as he untied his white double-ended dory. Pam was the first one in. She couldn't wait. The dory tipped precariously. Floyd chuckled.

"I see you brought a bunch of landlubbers with you, Sharm," he said.

"Step in the center," Gramp told Nancy, "and she won't tip." Nancy did as she was told. Then Gramp and Floyd got in. Floyd rowed with little short strokes—standing up and facing the way he was going as most men in these parts did.

"Don't know if Barnabas is to home," he said, when they were halfway to the island. "He's set out some traps lately, turned lobsterman since the government discontinued the light. Lighthouse keepers seem to be going out of fashion. The government sold him the island cheap."

"We'll chance it," said Gramp.

They wove in and out among the pot buoys

and the boats. Soon they were close to Indian Island. There wasn't any landing place on the island. Only great pink rocks with the surf piling up on them. But Floyd rowed them around to the sea side and into a cleft in the rocks filled with yellow scum from the waves. The dory slid in on a wave.

"Jump out," said Floyd. And Nancy jumped out onto a rock at the right time when the boat was up close on the wave. Then the wave receded and the dory with it.

"You next, Pam," said Gramp.

The dory washed in on the next wave.

"Now?" asked Pam. But by the time she had said "now" the dory was already on its way out.

"I'll say 'go' when you should jump," said Floyd.

The next wave came.

"Go," cried Floyd.

Pam hesitated a moment, screwing up her courage. Then she jumped. She shouldn't have hesitated, for she jumped just a second too late.

She landed on the rock but not far enough on. Where she landed was slippery and wet with slime that the sun had not yet dried. Pam slipped down the rock, clutched at another one horny with barnacles, lost her grip, and slid into the water. With all her clothes on. When the next wave came in Gramp leaped out. Pam was treading water with all her might and her brown eyes were round and frightened.

"Give me your hand," Gramp said. Pam held out her hand. Gramp grabbed it and pulled her out.

"Okay," he called to Floyd. "Thanks a lot." Floyd rowed against the waves, pulled the dory into open water, and headed back toward the mainland.

"That didn't scare you, Pam, did it?" Gramp asked with his arm about her shoulders.

"No," said Pam, with chattering teeth. It was cold in the wind now that she was wet. "I'm just afraid I won't know what to tell Aunt Ivory when she sees me such a mess."

"Let's forget about that and cross our bridges when we come to them," said Gramp. "They'll have some dry clothes for you up to the house."

Pam smiled and looked up the rocks to where the whitewashed, stone house sat with its back to the spruce trees and its face to the sea.

"Oh," she said softly. The three of them clambered up the rocks and up over the tan field of soft dead hay, through the prickly sprays of juniper and the stiff bristles of blueberry plants. Two cedars and a solitary tamarack stood guard on the hill. They reached the house beside the lighthouse and Gramp knocked at the door. Some footsteps came running. Pam and Nancy held their breath. The door opened. And there stood the mistress of the house.

CHAPTER FOUR

The House on Indian Island

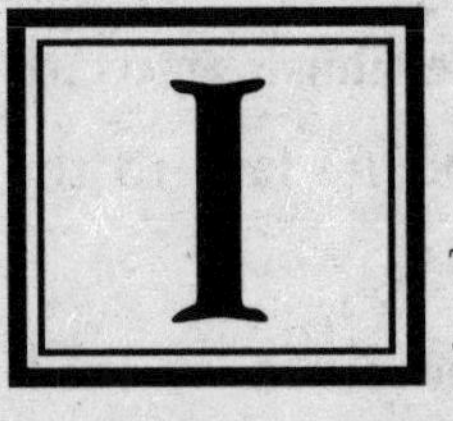

T WAS PENNY.

"Oh," she said. "It's Pamela. Barney!" she called. "It's Pamela."

But she need not have called, for Barney was already grinning around from behind her back. He couldn't contain himself.

"You're the twin!" he exploded. "I knew it the minute you took your hat off in the Ferris wheel."

"No, you didn't," Penny said. "You weren't really sure until you heard her aunt call her Pamela *Kellyhorn*."

"I am the twin, I guess," said Pam. "Oh," she said, "I forgot. This is Nancy and Gramp—Penny and Barney."

Four how-do-you-do's followed.

"Barnabas home?" asked Gramp. He wasn't, but Penny said he'd be back soon. She invited them all into the parlor. They stepped over the granite doorstep. All except Pam, that is. She was standing and shivering in a puddle of drip. In the excitement of meeting they had forgotten her wet clothes.

"I can't come in. I'm all wet. I fell in," she explained.

"Well, come on in. I'll get you something dry," said Penny.

Pam stepped into the little entry hall. It was a one-and-a-half-story house. A doorway to the right disclosed the kitchen "and everything" as Barney explained. This took up half the ground floor. To the left was the parlor which was half as large as the kitchen. A door in the parlor opened into a bedroom which took up the remaining space on the ground floor. "Puppa's room," Penny told them, when she ushered them into the parlor. She jerked up the shades. The parlor was very seldom used. But today was a special occasion.

"Please sit down," she said politely. And gingerly and just as politely Nancy and Gramp settled themselves on the horsehair loveseat beside a rickety old melodeon. It was a room to act gingerly in—filled with the treasures that Barnabas's grandfather had brought back from his sailing voyages. Pink and fluted shells decorated the mantelpiece; at either end sat thin porcelain vases filled with sweeping decorative grasses. "A special kind of hay," Barney explained as he sat down to play host while Penny took Pam to get some dry clothes.

"Where is your room?" Pam asked Penny as they left the parlor.

"There," said Penny, pointing to a rope ladder which hung from a hatch in the ceiling of the entry hall. She started up the ladder and Pam followed. Under the roof was one large room divided in two by a wall of old sail canvas.

"That's Barney's half and this is mine,"

Penny said, as she took Pam into the east half. There was a window in the gable end of the room on one side of which was a built-in bookcase half-filled with well-thumbed schoolbooks and just as well-thumbed books that Penny read for pleasure on rainy days. The rest of the shelves in the bookcase were filled with a collection of sea urchins of all sizes, a gull's spotted, brown egg, a crane's light blue egg, a piece of red jasper, shining flakes of mica, and a stone that looked strangely like a witch's head.

"I just can't help collecting junk," Penny explained. "It's like a disease."

On the other side of the window was a built-in closet. Between the bookcase and the closet and under the window was Penny's bed. Only it was a built-in bunk, covered with a red and blue patchwork quilt. It looked like one of Aunt Ivory's patterns, Pam thought.

"On good days," Penny said, "I can just lie in bed in the morning and see all the way across Penobscot Bay to Isle au Haut."

"Oh," said Pam, her eyes shining.

Penny opened the closet and got out a shirt, a faded pair of overalls and an old pair of sneakers.

"I'd like to give you a dress but I don't have any," she said, as she handed Pam the clothes.

"Penny," called Barney's voice from below the hatch. "I'm going to show them the lighthouse. Maybe you'd better come along because you understand better about how it used to work than I do."

"Okay. Will you be all right, Pam?"

"Sure," said Pam. Penny went over to the hatch. She paused and grinned at Pam. "I'm sure glad you're my twin," she said, before she lowered herself down the rope ladder.

Pam sat on the edge of Penny's bunk and pulled on the faded, blue overalls. So far everything was fine. Penny *was* her twin. And nobody had said anything about Barnabas having another wife. Surely they would have seen her if she were in the house. It was the nicest house she had ever seen. Everything was quiet now. Only a fly trying to find his way out of the window broke the silence. Pam put on the sneakers. They fitted perfectly. And then she heard someone below. *Galump. Galump.* It was the sound of rubber boots. They were in the kitchen. She heard the person walk over to the sink, then the creak of the pump and the sound of water gushing out of it. It was quiet again. The person must have been drinking the water, for a minute later she heard a loud masculine "Ahhhhhhh" as though the water had tasted good. It was the voice of a man, but it wasn't Gramp's voice. Besides, he didn't have rubber boots on. Pam didn't make a sound. She would wait until whoever it was had gone. The boots walked across the kitchen. She couldn't hear them any longer. Pam tied her sneakers and walked across to the hatch. She lowered herself down the rope ladder. From the kitchen came a rhythmical crunch, crunch. Pam jumped off the bottom rung of the ladder.

"That you, Barney?" called a deep voice.

"Barney's in the lighthouse," she answered.

"Come here," said the voice.

Pam came. She stood on the threshold of the kitchen. Rocking in the Boston rocker by the stove was one of the largest men Pam had ever seen. His red eyebrows bristled at Pam, but the eyes beneath them were startlingly blue and friendly. His hair was red too, and he had a wide red mustache that moved with the smile that spread across his bony face. And the smile stretched wider than the mustache. He was a large man but he didn't have an extra ounce of fat on him. His long legs were dressed in blue denim pants, and on his feet were the largest, blackest rubber boots Pam had ever seen. A discolored yellow oilskin jacket hung on the back of the rocker. All in all he was extraordinary—the kind of man you liked instantly and didn't forget easily. Pam hesitated on the threshold. He was such a *large* man.

"Come here," he said again. "Haven't you got a kiss for your Puppa? You haven't seen him yet today. You and Barney were still sawing wood when I left at four this morning."

Pam had a moment of indecision. And then a vast idea presented itself. This was Barnabas—this was her father. He thought she was Penny. She wanted to fly into his arms and tell him all about it. But she restrained herself. She was laughing inside. Her own father couldn't tell her from her sister. This is going to be wonderful, she thought. And Pam walked over to the rocker and kissed her father for the first time in her life as if nothing out of the ordinary had happened.

"Look," Barnabas said. He had the new fall and winter Sears-Roebuck catalogue in his lap. It was open to the section containing girls' clothing. "You ought to have a dress now that you are twelve. I can't have you going to school in pants any longer. You can help pick it out."

Pam's face was all crinkled up in the pleasure of the joke she was playing. But Barnabas thought she was smiling because she was pleased he was going to get her a dress. It surprised him because Penny scorned dresses.

"On page one fifty-seven is one I like," said Pam. It was a dress that Pam had been teasing Aunt Ivory to get her, and she was sure Penny would like it. A red plaid dress with a round white collar.

"Hmmmm," said Barnabas. "That's right pretty. Get a string and we'll measure."

String, thought Pam, string? Where would string be? Heavenly Nellie, she was going to be found out. She looked around the kitchen. There wasn't any string anywhere.

"We ought to own a tape measure if we're going to start buying dresses," said Barnabas. "String will do, though." Then he added, "There's some extra mackerel line in the top drawer of that dresser. That'll do. There's a ruler there too."

Saved! thought Pam, as she got the equipment.

"Now, let's see how we do this," said

Barnabas. He turned to the back of the catalogue to find out how to measure. They measured Pam twice to be sure, and then they measured the string and they figured out that Pam took a size fourteen, which Pam knew all the time anyhow but she couldn't let on. Barnabas got out the order blank and he had just finished writing down the necessary information and was licking the envelope when Penny and Barney and Gramp and Nancy emerged from the lighthouse shouting and laughing.

"Who is that mob, anyhow?" asked Barnabas. The mob entered the kitchen.

"Gramp Drake!" shouted Barnabas. "Well, I'll be a smoked eel! Where did you come from?" And he grabbed Gramp's hand in his big bony one and pumped it up and down. Then he saw Penny. He stopped shaking Gramp's hand which was pretty well exercised by that time anyway. He slapped himself on the forehead. "For the love of Crow Pete! Am I getting tetched in the haid or what?" He looked at Pam and then back at Penny. "It's Pamela," he said looking at Penny. "My little Pamela! I thought I'd never see you again. I'll bet Ivory doesn't know about this trip." And he hugged Penny and squeezed her until she hadn't any breath left and all she could do was wink back at Pam who was winking vigorously so that the rest of them would catch on. Then Barnabas hugged Pam and called her Penny and they danced around so much that soon only the twins knew which was which. Because, you see, Pam had brushed back her wet bangs, and now there was no difference between them except a few small freckles on Penny's nose.

"Food," shouted Barnabas. "That's what we want. Come on, you women, feed us men. We'll go sit in the sun, we men, eh, little Barnabas?" he said, and he put an arm around Barney's shoulders, "while you get together some grub."

Pam's heart turned over. "Little Barnabas." That must mean Barney was a junior. But as soon as the men left the room, the conversation began to buzz.

"First," asked Nancy, "who is who?"

Pam and Penny explained, truthfully this time.

"You can tell by the freckles on Penny's nose," said Pam. It was the only difference. They were laughing hysterically.

"Let's get dinner in a hurry, and afterward Barney and I will show you the secret clubhouse," said Penny.

"And then we can lay plans," said Nancy.

"For what?" asked Penny.

"We'll tell you later," said Pam. "Let's hurry. There isn't much time left, because we promised Aunt Ivory we'd be back early."

So they hurried. They hurried with the cooking and the eating and the dishes, and if they didn't have indigestion it was only because they were young enough not to. Soon the girls and Barney were running over the brown needles in the spruce woods and over the brow of the hill. From the top they could see Abbidydumkeag's wharves and the white boats and men rowing dories in and out of the pot buoys. The land fell away beneath them into steep rocks at the bottom of which the waves broke into white foam.

"I'll lead the way," said Penny, overruling Barney. They scrambled down the rocks following the devious course of the toe holds that Penny and Barney had discovered for themselves. Just above the high-water mark they came to a flat rock which they had not been able to see from above because it lay beneath a jutting cliff. Long ago when the island had been formed, long before men had lived, this one, single, solid cliff had been split in two and this split formed a narrow corridor through which they followed Penny. About thirty feet in it seemed to come to an end. But to the left was a small opening formed by a slanting boulder. Penny got down on her hands and knees and crawled through. The rest followed.

"This is it," said Penny. "This is the clubhouse." It was a small cave that couldn't have held any more than the four of them. It was dark and dank and a shaft of mysterious, green light pierced through a cleft in the rock. The only other light came from the opening through which they had crawled. They began to lay their plans.

"Before we do anything else we have to know whether Barnabas—I mean, our father—is married again," said Pam.

"After Mumma died, he never had another wife," Penny told them.

"Well, what about Barney? How does he happen to be named Barnabas too?"

"He's like a brother," Penny said, "but he's really my—our—cousin. His father, Uncle Conrad, is Puppa's brother. He's in the circus. For some reason he never comes to Abbidydumkeag. But he wanted Barney to be brought up on Indian Island the way he was. Besides, he says the circus is no life for a child."

"Dad does a flying act," Barney said proudly. Pam and Nancy nodded their heads though they had no notion what a "flying act" was. But of course they couldn't admit that to Barney.

"He feels pretty bad sometimes that he doesn't live with his real father," Penny whispered in Pam's ear.

"I'm glad he isn't a junior though," said Pam. And she told Penny and Barney about Aunt Ivory and Barnabas and their mother, and Barney's eyes popped as he drank it in. "I knew there was something in it the *minute* I saw you at the fair," he crowed.

"If only your aunt Ivory and Puppa would get married, we'd all be together the way we ought to be. There's no point in having a twin if you never see her," said Penny.

"That's our plan," said Pam. "But we don't know how to do it."

"Maybe you wouldn't be happy here," said Barney. "It's an awful lot of trouble rowing into the village each morning to school. Part of the time we can't go when it's extra rough. And then we have to make it up later."

"Oh, I'd love it," said Pam. "I wouldn't mind missing school a bit."

"But," said practical Nancy, "maybe you really wouldn't like it. There are lots of things that sound nice but really aren't when you come right down to it. Like walking in the rain. Or wading in a brook in the woods in the summer. That *sounds* nice, but the mosquitoes are as big as birds and nearly eat you to death."

"I'm sure I'd like it," Pam insisted.

"And," Nancy went on, "maybe Penny wouldn't like Aunt Ivory for a mother."

"Oh, I'm sure she would," said Pam. "Aunt Ivory's wonderful. Sometimes she's cross but that's only because she's lonely and she wouldn't be if she were married to Barnabas—I mean, Puppa." It was hard to say "Puppa." The word was still new to her.

"I know," said Nancy, who adored Aunt

Ivory. "But maybe first you ought to try it out."

"But how?" asked the twins in one breath.

"Well, it worked today. Your own father couldn't tell you apart. Why doesn't Pam stay here and pretend she's Penny? And Penny can come back with us and stay for a couple of weeks, and then Gramp can bring you back and we can talk about it again. If you still want to go ahead with the plans, why then it would be fine."

"We can call it the Period of Trial," said Barney officially.

"Do you think it could possibly work?" asked Pam.

"Well, it won't hurt to try," said Penny. "I'm game if you are."

"All right," said Pam. And they shook hands. "Besides," Pam added, "if they do discover it, we don't have to say why we did it. Neither of them would like to think we were butting in. And if it does work out it will make Aunt Ivory happy."

"And Puppa too," added Penny. "He gets awful lonely."

"And me," said Pam.

"And me," said Penny.

They had been there a long while and the sun was getting low when they emerged from the cave. Already the tide had come in considerably. It had nearly reached the high-water mark on the rocks. They scrambled up the cliffs and over the top of the hill, through the woods and back to the house.

"We were just about to come looking for you," said Barnabas. "But I thought it would be kind of useless. I never can find you when you're in your hide-out."

"Better get on your dress, Pam," said Gramp to both Penny and Pam just so that he wouldn't make a mistake. The girls climbed up through the hatch. They were a long time up there because the twins had to give each other some last-minute tips.

"Anyhow," Nancy pointed out, "Barney can

help Pam get over the rough spots, and I'll try to be around as much as possible so that Aunt Ivory won't think Pam has forgotten everything she taught her."

"Hey, you girls, hurry up!" called Gramp up the hatch.

"Bangs!" cried Nancy in dismay. "Penny, we've got to cut you some bangs. Quick!"

Penny got some scissors and Nancy started snipping. "Come on," called Gramp.

Nancy snipped faster. Finally she combed the bangs triumphantly. But anyone could see that they had been cut in a hurry.

"We haven't time to straighten them. They'll have to do. Pull down the hat that Aunt Ivory makes you wear and no one will notice," said Pam.

"I'll fix them up tomorrow," said Nancy.

The three girls lowered themselves down the rope ladder. Pam had pinned back her bangs with bobby pins and no one but Nancy and Barney was the wiser. Barnabas rowed them

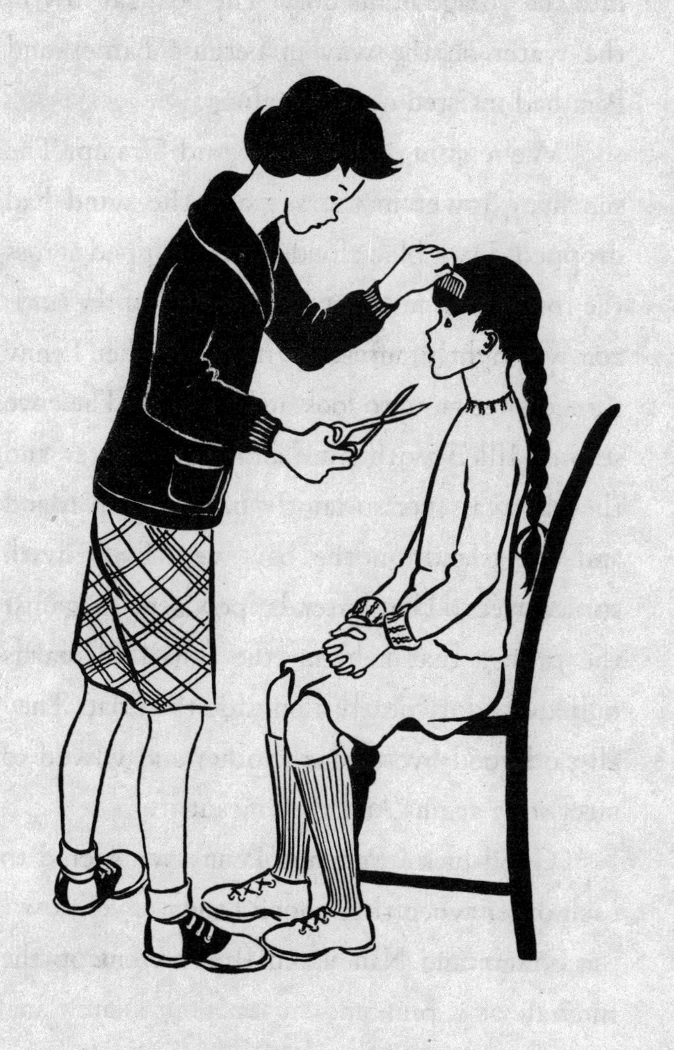

into the village in his dory. The boat sat low in the water on the way in because Barney and Pam had insisted on going along.

"We're going to be late," said Gramp. The sun hung lower in the sky and the wind had dropped. Dark blue clouds were stripped across the rosy sunset in the west. The rest of the horizon was lightly suffused with pink when Penny turned once more to look at her home. The cove seemed filled with pink and green water and the bay was ever so faintly blue. Indian Island and the islands in the bay were black with spruce trees. The water lapped gently against the pilings that held up the wharf. Barnabas pulled his dory neatly alongside the float. They all said good-bye to one another and vowed to meet soon again. And they meant it.

"Good luck," Pam and Penny whispered to each other when they shook hands.

Gramp and Nancy and Penny went up the runway.

"Good-bye," they called.

"Good-bye," called Barnabas and Barney and Pam from below.

"Glad to see you in a dress again, Pam," Pam heard Gramp say to Penny as they walked up the runway. "It was pretty confusing out on Indian."

Pam chuckled to herself. Even Gramp, that wise old owl, was fooled.

CHAPTER FIVE

The Striped Cat

HE TRUCK STOPPED with a jerk at 11 Elm Street.

"Tell your aunt Ivory I'm sorry we're so late, Pam," said Gramp to Penny as she climbed out of the truck. "Tell her I was chewing the fat with someone, if you want. But better not tell her who. I hope she doesn't notice your clothes. You don't look like the same neat girl who got in the truck this morning."

Penny did look rather rumpled. She couldn't help smiling, because she wasn't the same neat girl who had climbed into the truck that morning though Gramp didn't know it.

"Good luck," Nancy called as Gramp put the truck in first. And she didn't mean on account of the clothes either. Penny suddenly had cold feet. She wanted to turn back to the truck, explain everything, and get Gramp to take her back to Indian Island. But the truck had started, and with it went her last chance of backing out.

She turned and looked at her new home. Elm Street ran up the hill at a right angle to Main Street. A row of towering elm trees marched down either side of it. A hundred feet back from the road sat Number 11. It was a small, white house with pointed, Gothic windows and a steep roof decorated with fanciful jigsaw curlicues. Two ladylike hemlocks in sweeping, green skirts stood on either side of the tidy gravel path that led up to the front door.

It was dark out now—nearly six o'clock. The glow of the sunset had almost disappeared and the sky was a pale green at the horizon—a sign that it would be cold tomorrow. Penny walked up the path to the front door. A window was set into the top half of the door and squares of red and green and amber glass ran around the edge of it. She looked at the white-knobbed bellpull and would have pulled it until she remembered that she was meant to be Pam and this was where she lived and people just walked into their own houses. She opened the door. As she did so, something white streaked by her into the dark. And then another something and then another until at last five of them had swished out the door. Penny saw the last of them. They were white cats. Five of them. Five white cats. She had better get them before Aunt Ivory discovered that she had let them out. Penny turned and went running down the path. She had left the front door open and in the light from the hall she saw the last cat's tail disappear behind a bush. Penny followed them. The cats disappeared through a hole in the hedge at the side of the house. Penny followed. Leaves were in her hair and twigs caught in her big thick sweater. She stood up. No sooner had she started running again than she fell over a rock. But it wasn't a rock. When she sat up and looked around for the cats, she discovered that she was in a graveyard and that she had tripped over a gravestone. From the far end of the graveyard by a tall cedar hedge came a mewing. Dimly she could discern the white animals moving among the pale gravestones. She shook herself, stood up, and went over to them. They didn't run away from her any longer. Two of them were even sitting down. They seemed to have found what they were looking for. By the light of the moon above the cedars Penny saw a sixth cat in the far corner behind an old, slanting, lichen-covered stone. He was crying pitifully as he lay in a nest trampled down in the unclipped grass on the forgotten grave. Penny squatted beside the cat and stroked his head. Something sticky met her touch. She saw that there were dark bloodstains on the striped fur. His wounds will have to be cleaned, Penny told herself. She picked the cat up in her arms

BARBARA

and walked carefully with him through the wrought-iron gate of the cemetery, along Elm Street, and turned up the path of Number 11. The five white cats followed in her wake.

"Pamela Kellyhorn!" came a voice from the doorway. It was the same voice Penny had heard at the fair. It was Aunt Ivory's voice. She stood in the doorway silhouetted against the light from the hall with arms akimbo. "Whatever have you been up to running around in the dark and leaving the hall door open so that the cats got out while I was in the midst of fixing their supper?"

"They're right behind me now," said Penny, as she reached the door. "And I've got a hurt cat in my arms," she said, proffering the wounded animal to Aunt Ivory. Even without the nasty bloodstains, the cat would not have been a pretty one. He was a striped gray cat—long and thin with a pointed face and scraggly fur—the kind of cat that lives from garbage can to garbage can and never knows from which can his next meal is coming. A homeless cat with nothing to recommend him in the way of looks but a wide pair of appealing, green eyes. If Aunt Ivory wouldn't take him in, Penny told herself, she would go to Gramp the next morning and ask him to take her back to Indian Island. Aunt Ivory had no idea that she was on trial. She held forth her arms.

"You poor little cat," she said, though the cat was large and long. She took him in her arms without once noticing Penny's clothes. "Come in and shut the door behind you, Pam," she told Penny. "There's some supper waiting for you on the kitchen table."

Penny followed her into the kitchen. Aunt Ivory put the cat gently down on an old quilt behind the stove while Penny sat down at the table to a big plate of baked beans and boiled potatoes and steaming, moist brown bread. That's right, she remembered, it is only Saturday still. An awful lot had happened since morning. As she ate she watched Aunt Ivory.

Aunt Ivory looked very pretty and very young in the blue dress that matched her eyes. Though she wore her light gold hair drawn tightly back into a bun, wisps of curls escaped around the edge of her forehead. And her cheeks were pink. She bustled around putting the kettle on to boil and getting clean rags to wash the cat's wounds.

"Do you think it was a dog that got him?" asked Penny.

"Looks like it," replied Aunt Ivory. "Probably the horrid yellow dog belonging to that Rusty Hanna up the hill. Every animal he has he mistreats. He kicks his dogs. No wonder they get nasty and bite everyone. The Cushman boy won't even get out of the truck up there anymore. He's been bitten three times already. They say it was pitiful the way Rusty beat and prodded his oxen at the fair. And that you should have seen his face when he only got third. You can't get anywhere that way. Look at Hiram Crimmins. He came in first, and all he used were soft words. His oxen were smaller too. Must admit," she said, and she blushed, "I wasn't too pleased to get second with my quilt. But at least I acted like a lady. When I heard them talking about Rusty down to the store this morning I made up my mind to stop acting so silly and as soon as I came home I got out the ragbag." She tossed her head as she tore a white rag in two for a bandage. "Next fall, Pam," she said, "the Uxton Fair is going to see the most beautiful quilt that has ever been seen around here. And I'm going to make it."

Heaped in the rocker across from the table were the gay contents of the ragbag—scraps of old-fashioned, sprigged calico, shiny pieces of sateen, pink muslin (which Penny discovered later was left over from the ruffle around Pam's bed), Turkey red, green linen—all the odds and ends of dresses and curtains and aprons that Aunt Ivory had collected during her uneventful ladyhood.

"Are you going to work on it after supper?" Penny asked.

"After we've fixed up the cat. If you've finished your supper, you can hold him while I wash his cuts."

Penny jumped up and carried her dishes to the sink before she picked up the cat and sat carefully down with him in her lap. Aunt Ivory washed away the blood with the water from the kettle and soon the cuts were clean. The cat looked much better, although there was a nasty open cut on his back and a hole right through his ear. Every so often he mewed pitifully when it hurt especially. And once he dug his claws right through Penny's skirt. When it was over, Penny put the cat back behind the stove on the quilt, and Aunt Ivory gave him a saucer of milk which he greedily lapped up. Before long the dishes were washed, and Penny and Aunt Ivory sat down on the floor with the contents of the ragbag spread out between them.

"First we ought to decide on the color scheme," said Aunt Ivory.

"How about blue?" asked Penny. "Everyone

likes blue—the blue sky and the blue water."

"And blue shirts and overalls and wagons," said Aunt Ivory.

"To match the blue ribbon for first prize," added Penny.

"We ought to have red just in case it gets second prize. Which it won't," said Aunt Ivory.

Penny nodded. "Everyone likes red too." She was thinking of the red plaid dress she had noticed in the Sears-Roebuck catalogue. Not that she liked *dresses*, but that was a pretty one.

Aunt Ivory agreed. She was thinking about a red dress that Barnabas had once told her she looked beautiful in.

They had just decided on blue and red when a knock sounded on the kitchen door.

"Who can that be?" asked Aunt Ivory. "It's nearly nine o'clock. Almost bedtime."

"It's Saturday night, though," reminded Penny. For on Saturday nights everyone in the outlying districts came to town to gossip on the street corners or to go to the movies. There were always westerns on Saturday nights. Whole families would turn out—women with sleeping babies in their arms and men in clean shirts. Little boys chased each other up and down the sidewalk with ice-cream cones in their hands and ice cream on their faces; little girls strolled in and out of the big people with their arms about each other's waists. Older boys and girls laughed and talked excitedly together. That was the way it was in Abbidydumkeag, Penny knew, and in Twidboro and all the other towns.

"So it is," said Aunt Ivory, as she got up from the floor and straightened herself. It wouldn't do for the village people to see Ivory Perry sitting on the floor. She opened the door.

"Evening, Rusty," she said politely. It was Rusty Hanna. He was a medium-sized, unkempt man with a shock of sandy hair and that unpleasant kind of palely freckled, pink skin which is covered with little, rough specks like goose pimples—except that goose pimples went away and these never did. His eyebrows, if he had any, were invisible and his mean little eyes, set close together in his head, were fringed with white eyelashes. It gave him a naked look which was only increased by a small, weak mouth. Penny disliked him immediately.

"What can I do for you?" Aunt Ivory continued politely. But she stood in front of him with her hand on the doorknob so that he couldn't get into the house without pushing her aside.

"Somebody downstreet saw your girl come in the house with my cat in her arms." The man swayed slightly. Evidently he had been drinking. Aunt Ivory braced herself and stood her ground even more firmly.

"It must have been one of my own cats," she said.

"It wasn't a white cat," Rusty Hanna snapped.

"It was dark when Pamela came in," Aunt Ivory pointed out. "Whoever saw her might have been mistaken."

"No they weren't." Rusty was belligerent. "My cat's here. I know he is. The durned critter's been gone for three days and the rats are eating my hens. I'm not going to leave this house without him." He attempted to push past Aunt Ivory.

She stood her ground. "I said your cat wasn't here," she repeated. As she said it a mewing came from behind the stove.

"You're a liar," Rusty snarled. From the porch came a vicious growl. "Even the dog knows you're lying."

Aunt Ivory's eyes flashed. No one had ever called her a liar before. She closed the door farther so that the yellow dog couldn't get in.

"That's one of my own cats crying," she retorted. Penny reached for one of the white cats that was sleeping under the table and prodded him forward across Rusty's line of vision.

"You see," said Aunt Ivory haughtily. With one hand she reached for the white cat and lifted him onto her shoulder. With the other hand she closed the door on the pale, nasty face. But Rusty's foot was in the door.

"You're still lying," he sneered. But Aunt Ivory had won a victory. "I'll be back," he added ominously as he removed his foot from the door.

Aunt Ivory shut the door and slid the bolt. They could hear him thumping down the steps. The dog followed barking.

"Will you fix the front door, Pam?" Aunt Ivory said. "We'd better lock up tonight."

Penny did as she was told. When she came back Aunt Ivory was sitting on the floor with the rags scattered before her.

"It was red and blue, wasn't it, that we decided on?" she asked, as though nothing had happened. Penny squatted down opposite her.

"Yes," she replied, smiling broadly. Aunt Ivory was certainly proving herself to be a lot more than a nice lady.

She'd be just the right kind of a woman for Puppa, Penny thought as she started putting the red rags in one pile and the blue in another.

CHAPTER SIX

11 *Elm Street*

THE DELIGHTFUL breakfast smell of bacon and coffee crept under the door. Time to get up. But Penny didn't open her eyes. The room was cold, and she huddled under the warm quilt appreciating her bed. She kept her eyes closed for several minutes and lay there speculating as to whether the weather would be clear enough for her to see across Penobscot Bay to Vinalhaven and Isle au Haut. The cold air coming in the window across her bed was damp, so evidently the wind had shifted and she wouldn't be able to. Finally she opened the one eye that was outside the covers. A puddle of water lay on the window sill and silver beads of rain hung on the screen. Penny sat up in bed. But it wasn't Penobscot Bay she saw. It was a little yard and a cedar hedge and on the other side of the hedge a cemetery with neat, white gravestones and brown leaves matted with rain on the graves. Beyond this was a white meetinghouse. For a moment Penny couldn't remember where she was. And then it all came back to her—Pam's arrival at Indian Island, the conference in the cave, the new bangs, the trip back in the truck with Nancy and Gramp, the five white cats and the striped one in the graveyard, and finally Rusty Hanna threatening Aunt Ivory.

Penny scrambled out of bed and into her underwear. Then she went over to the washstand and poured water out of the pitcher into the washbowl. Everything in Pam's room was pink and white. The white pitcher and bowl had pink roses painted on them, and the mug holding Pam's pink toothbrush did too. Penny washed her face and poured water over the toothbrush so that it would look used. Then she opened the closet door. Pam's dresses were neatly hanging in a row. Penny selected a navy blue one—a prim, tidy dress that looked like Sunday. When she had it on she braided her pigtails and combed her bangs, and the face that looked back at her from the mirror would have taken an expert more clever than Barnabas or Aunt Ivory to say whether it was Pam or Penny. Then she went downstairs. Aunt Ivory didn't hear her coming. She was kneeling in the center of the big, round braided rug in the kitchen. The smallest of the white cats was standing on his hind legs beside her trying to get a piece of meat which she held aloft in one hand. The other cats sat at attention around the edge of the rug facing her.

"All right, James. Around, boy," she said to the cat in the center. As she said it she moved the hand that held the piece of meat in a circle until the meat was behind her. Then she changed hands and continued the circle. The cat followed the piece of meat, walking around

Aunt Ivory on his hind legs all the time. When he had completed the circle Aunt Ivory tossed the meat into the air and James caught it with a snap of his jaws. Penny watched from the threshold of the kitchen door, her mouth open in amazement. Aunt Ivory looked up.

"I'm teaching them a new trick, Pam," she said. "I want to get them all walking on their hind legs in a circle at the same time. James has been the hardest to teach. But suddenly this morning he seems to have caught onto it. The next step is to get them all to do it at once.

"Help yourself to breakfast and sit down. I didn't wait for you. I thought you ought to sleep a little late this morning." Aunt Ivory turned back to the cats while Penny got herself some oatmeal and sat down to breakfast. Penny couldn't take her eyes off Aunt Ivory and the cats. She watched them over the rim of her glass of milk. One after the other they left their sitting position and walked around Aunt Ivory. Finally it came to James's turn again. By the time all five of them had done it without a mistake Penny had finished her breakfast.

"All right, boys," Aunt Ivory said. "That's enough for today." She tossed them each an extra morsel of meat as a bonus.

"Come on, Pam," she said. "Let's hurry through the dishes and the beds. It's almost time for church."

"You know," she added, while they were doing the dishes, "I really shouldn't practice with the cats on Sunday. But if I miss a day I'm afraid they'll forget."

That Sunday was the first time Penny had ever been in an old-fashioned meetinghouse. The pews fascinated her. They were in the shape of little boxes. Penny followed Aunt Ivory down the aisle and into one of these little stalls where the pews were so arranged that some people even had to sit with their backs to the minister. The pews were so small that when they were full everybody's knees were crowded against the other fellow's. The pew they sat in was already almost full. So Aunt Ivory sat frontward and Penny backward with her knees touching Aunt Ivory's.

The minister spoke in a singsong manner that Penny found difficult to listen to. Especially because she had her back to him. She tried to concentrate on what he was saying. But the harder she tried the less she heard until finally she gave it up altogether and began wondering whether Aunt Ivory would notice how crooked her bangs were when they were sitting facing each other at such close quarters. But Aunt Ivory's head was tilted back and her eyes rested on the pulpit. Penny looked at her and decided that she was gluing her eyes on the pulpit in a desperate effort to stay awake. Penny forgot her bangs and looked around the church for Nancy. She saw her toward the back tucked away behind a lot of people in dark Sunday clothes. On one side of her sat a handsome woman who looked the way Nancy probably would in thirty years or so. That would be her mother, Penny decided. On the other side of Nancy was Gramp. He was fast asleep and Nancy was tugging at his sleeve. He opened one eye, and then he blinked and shook his head trying to wake up. But he found it impossible and almost immediately was asleep again. This time his mouth was open and undoubtedly he was snoring, though Penny was too far away to hear him above the droning of the minister. Nancy was grinning, and Mrs. Drake—for it must have been she—looked at him with a little frown and then looked back at the pulpit and pretended she didn't know him. Penny caught Nancy's eye and they exchanged grins. Nancy mouthed some words that Penny couldn't make out but she figured that Nancy wanted to speak to her after church.

After a long time the sermon ended and the recessional hymn started wheezing out of the old organ. Penny edged out of the pew behind Aunt Ivory. Everyone that Aunt Ivory said "How do" to Penny smiled at because they were all probably friends of Pam's. Nancy was standing on the steps of the meetinghouse with her mother and Gramp and a lot of other people when Aunt Ivory and Penny finally reached the door. It was slow going. She had heard one man mutter, "Firetrap," on the way out. And another man answered, "Ayah, the place could be burnt to the ground before they could get even half the people out." Finally they reached the steps. The people with Gramp and Mrs. Drake all said, "Hi," to Aunt Ivory and Penny. Penny was afraid she would make a blunder if they had to stop to pass the time of day.

"Morning," said Aunt Ivory, and she went over to them. Penny had to follow. Nancy grabbed her and said, "Come on." She was afraid Penny would say something wrong too.

"We're going to walk home, Mumma," she called.

"All right, dear," said Mrs. Drake.

"Now, concentrate," Nancy told Penny, when she got her to the bottom of the steps.

"I don't think I'll ever be able to concentrate again after that minister," Penny said.

"Wasn't he awful?" Nancy agreed. "He's not the regular one. The Twidboro minister is out of town. It's too bad the first Sunday you're here you couldn't hear him. He's a regular guy. But that's aside from the point. Turn around, Penny, and act casual while I point out the people you should know."

Penny turned around.

"You know Gramp," Nancy said. "And that's my mother talking to your aunt. The man on the furthest left is my father, only usually he wears a white jacket because he runs the drugstore down street. The big man he's talking to is Hiram Crimmins. Besides having the strongest oxen in the county he's the town clerk. That mild-looking man in the pepper-and-salt suit she's talking to is the cleverest lawyer in the county, Mr. Harrowscratch. And that man in the fancy suit talking to the old woman is Mr. Coffin, the undertaker. He's probably asking her in to look over his parlor. There are three undertakers in Twidboro and the competition's something fierce."

Penny shuddered while she concentrated very hard. Especially on the faces, because they were all disguised in their Sunday best. They stood there ten minutes while Nancy pointed out to Penny the people she would be expected to know and told her little things about them that would help her remember. When Nancy was finished, Penny repeated their names until she had said them all correctly.

"I think that's about everyone you'll have to know," said Nancy. "Pam hasn't been here long enough to know them all."

The two girls turned and walked down the path and along the fence of the graveyard, past Aunt Ivory's house and three doors up to the Drake's. They took a pair of scissors out to the Hen House, locked themselves in and straightened Penny's bangs. The rest of the hour before dinner, Nancy spent giving Penny pointers on how to behave. She even drew a map of the town for her showing her how to get to the post office and the grocery store and the drug store and where each of the people lived.

"And here's Mr. Coffin's funeral parlor. But I don't guess you'll need to know where that is for at least eighty years. I can't think of anything else right now," said Nancy. "If you're in doubt, just act shy. Pam is very shy with almost everyone."

I hope Pam isn't too shy with Puppa, Penny thought as she walked back to 11 Elm. Penny herself wasn't scared of anyone—at least, not of many people. But she admitted that she was a little scared being set down in Twidboro among strangers under the name of Pamela Kellyhorn. Anyhow, she reassured herself, I haven't made a blunder yet. Aunt Ivory never noticed the messy clothes or the crooked bangs. And I'm pretty good at acting as though I'd worn dresses all my life. She strutted up the path of Number 11 tossing her pigtails.

But she had crowed too soon. It happened at lunch. They were eating buttercrunch ice cream that Penny at the last minute had been sent to get down at Mr. Drake's drugstore. She had found it immediately with the aid of Nancy's map. Penny was eating the ice cream, mentally patting herself on the back for having said, "Good morning, Mr. Drake," as though he were an old-time friend, when Aunt Ivory looked up from her plate and said:

"Pamela, where did you get that ring?"

Penny looked down at the turquoise ring on her finger that Barnabas had given her on her twelfth birthday. What could she say? She couldn't think of anything.

"Pamela, I asked you where you got that ring?"

"I—I found it."

"Where did you find it?"

Penny tried quickly to recall Nancy's map. But only a blank came to her mind.

"You don't think I *stole* it, do you, Aunt

Ivory?" she asked. She was stalling for time to think of some place where she might have found it.

"No, I don't, Pamela. I know you wouldn't steal.

"But," Aunt Ivory continued, "I would like to know where you found it."

"I found it by the graveyard on my way home from church," Penny said. And she blushed because she had never been able to lie with a straight face.

"Well, it wouldn't be right to keep it," said Aunt Ivory, "without first trying to find the owner. After lunch I'll help you write out an ad to put in the lost-and-found column of the *Courier-Gazette*."

So after lunch they wrote out the ad and Aunt Ivory put Penny's ring in her strong box for safe keeping.

That had been the first in a series of blunders.

After Sunday dinner Nancy had come over

to do her homework with Penny. Fortunately they were both in the same grade at school. Fortunately, too, their schoolbooks were identical. But unfortunately, Penny's and Pam's respective classes were at different places in their textbooks. Pam was ahead of Penny in her History book, though in Spelling, Pam's class was several chapters behind Penny's class. The latter worked to Penny's advantage because she would be way ahead of the class. However, it was the other way around in the Arithmetic book. Pam's class was five chapters ahead of Penny's.

"Oh, dear," said Nancy when they discovered this. "That's too bad, because Pam is at the top of the class in Arithmetic."

Penny's face fell. Arithmetic came hard to her too. And spelling which she was naturally good at anyhow was the one thing that Pam's class was behind in. Penny looked out of the window and was glad that it was a gloomy day outside. Otherwise she would have minded more having to stay in and do homework. Then she buckled down to a chapter of atrocious problems with decimals. At the end of a long afternoon she was more confused than ever, and she still had History and English and Spelling to do. And a week of school days stretched terrifyingly ahead of her.

"Nancy," she said, "before you go home, draw me a plan of the seating arrangement at school so that at least I will know who is who even if I don't know decimals."

Needless to say, it was late when Penny went to bed that night. Between the dishes and her homework and memorizing the seating arrangement at school—not to mention all the excitement of the rest of the day and of Saturday too—Penny was exhausted and she was asleep as soon as her head hit the pillow.

CHAPTER SEVEN

Aunt Ivory and the Pistol

THE WEEK AT school was terrible. There had been that first morning when she had walked to school with Nancy. They were walking along scuffing through the leaves when another girl had joined them.

"Over your mad?" she had asked Penny, putting her arm around her waist. At first sight Penny didn't like her. She was pale and fat and her hair could have done with a shampoo. But she put her arm around the fat girl's waist because, though it seemed unlikely, perhaps this was a friend of Pam's. She wished she knew what she was meant to be mad about.

"Did you ask your aunt Ivory about what I told you?" the girl continued.

Penny still couldn't answer. If only Nancy would help her out!

"Pam doesn't carry tales, Imogene," Nancy said, stressing the name Imogene so that Penny would catch it. She wished she hadn't forgotten to tell Penny about Imogene.

"Nobody said anything about carrying tales," Imogene retorted. "What do you know about it anyhow?"

"I don't know anything about it," Nancy replied.

"You do too. Otherwise you wouldn't have mentioned it. Pam Kellyhorn," she said, turning on Penny, "I'm never going to tell you anything again."

Frankly, Penny didn't care. She said as much to Nancy when Imogene had walked ahead of them to catch up to a blond boy who, Nancy informed her, was president of the eighth grade. The blond boy didn't act overjoyed to see her either. Penny hoped that Imogene wouldn't even bother to speak to her again.

"Don't worry," said Nancy. "She'll come back. Nobody likes her. Pam is about the only person who is nice to her, and that's because she soft-soaps Aunt Ivory so much that Aunt Ivory encourages her to come over and play with Pam. And Pam is about the politest girl in town no matter what she thinks."

"What is it that she's supposed to have told me?" Penny asked.

"Oh, someone told her something about Aunt Ivory having a sad love affair."

"Does she know anything more?" Penny asked. "About me and Puppa?"

"I don't think so," Nancy answered. The school bell was ringing, so without any more talk they went in and took their seats in Miss Hinton's class.

The first morning had started badly. It didn't improve, although the first hour had been encouraging. That had been Spelling. Penny had spelled correctly "principal" and "principle" and "capitol" and "capital." Miss Hinton looked pleased. And once she had said, "I knew if you put your mind to it, Pamela, you could be a good speller." Evidently, Spelling was Pam's shaky study. The next hour, however, was History and Geography, and Penny knew none of the answers.

Luckily, the bell rang for recess before Miss Hinton could get around to her for the third time. As Nancy had predicted, Imogene came right up to Penny at recess and got her off in a corner alone. In one way this was good because it prevented Penny from making too many blunders with the other girls. But it was poor exchange to have to spend the fifteen precious minutes of recess off in a corner with Imogene Elliott. Especially when all of those fifteen minutes were spent listening to Imogene scold her for having told Nancy what was suddenly meant to have been a deep, dark secret. Penny laughed to herself thinking about how much more there was to know than Imogene suspected.

The worst hour of the day came after recess.

That was Arithmetic. Miss Hinton sprung a test on them. It had been a terribly difficult test, and the class groaned when Miss Hinton wrote the problems on the board in her big, round schoolteacher handwriting. Penny heard one boy whisper, "I bet even Pam Kellyhorn won't be able to do this." Penny looked at the long numbers and the fractions and the decimal points and fervently prayed under her breath that she would not let Pam's reputation down. Miss Hinton gave them each a piece of yellow scrap paper to figure on. Penny filled it full of numbers, trying desperately to get the answers to the problems—any answer, even if it were wrong, would look better than nothing. When the half hour was almost up, she wrote down her answers on the sheet of white paper, folded it once lengthwise, signed her name, and handed it in with the other papers. But she knew the answers couldn't be right. You can't *guess* the answers to problems full of decimal points. After lunch Miss Hinton handed back the papers. No one in the class had done very well. But none had done as badly as Penny.

"I would like to see you after class, Pamela," Miss Hinton said, when she handed back Penny's paper. The reason she said it was a round, red goose egg written under Penny's name. Imogene Elliott leaned over and saw it. She whispered to the girl next to her, and the girl whispered to a boy on the other side of her. The boy whistled and whispered, "If Pam Kellyhorn got a zero I guess the rest of us aren't so dumb after all." Penny's face got very red. Going to school in Twidboro was even worse than she had imagined.

At three o'clock Miss Hinton repeated her request. "Will Pamela Kellyhorn please remain after school?" The class strapped up their books and filed out leaving Penny alone with Miss Hinton.

"Come here, Pamela, and bring your Arithmetic test," ordered Miss Hinton, tapping on her desk with a long bony finger. "What's happened to you, Pamela?" she asked, as Penny laid the paper on the green blotter in front of Miss Hinton.

Penny looked at the red zero. And then she looked down at the floor.

"Nothing, I guess," she said. She felt her neck growing red. And her ears. She knew she was blushing. She tried to stop the blush as it spread over her cheeks and forehead. "Nothing," she repeated, raising her eyes to Miss Hinton's. Miss Hinton did not look fierce as she had expected. Rather, she looked perplexed.

"Was it that you spent too much time on Spelling?"

"Yes," said Penny. "That was it." She hadn't even opened the Spelling book.

"But," Miss Hinton continued, "that doesn't explain why you couldn't do the first five problems. They were all in last week's work."

Penny looked back at the floor. There was nothing she could say. But Miss Hinton was speaking again.

"I'm very disappointed in you, Pamela. You have been my best Arithmetic pupil until today. Now suddenly you have become the worst. I can't understand it."

"I'm sorry," Penny whispered. "I'll try to do better next time." She was nearly crying. If only she hadn't let Pam down she wouldn't have minded.

"That will be all, Pamela," said Miss Hinton. Penny turned back to her desk to get her books. She put the strap around them and started for the door when Miss Hinton spoke again.

"One thing I nearly forgot," she said. "Come here." Penny walked back to Miss Hinton's desk. She could see Miss Hinton's big feet through the hole in the center of the desk. They were twisted around the rungs of the chair in an awkward-looking manner.

"What is the meaning of this?" Miss Hinton asked. She was pointing her long pale finger at the signature on the outside of Penny's paper.

Penny's mouth fell open in dismay. The signature read: PENELOPE KELLYHORN, GRADE 7. "I just think it's a nice name," said Penny.

"Well, from now on sign your own name to your papers. Where would the world be if we all went around signing names we liked the sound of?" Miss Hinton snorted as though she had just said some thing very clever. "Good night, Pamela," she added, as Penny made for the door.

"Good night, Miss Hinton," Penny said. And she heaved a sigh of relief when she got outside.

Tuesday had not been much better than Monday, or Wednesday than Tuesday. Each day Penny had been asked to stay after school to go over her Arithmetic problems with Miss Hinton. And each day Miss Hinton had become more puzzled and exasperated. No wonder then that Penny sighed with relief and hurried to catch up with Nancy when on Friday, Miss Hinton did not ask her to remain after school.

The two girls scuffed leisurely home through the leaves with two days of no school stretching pleasantly ahead of them.

"I'm glad Aunt Ivory asked you for supper and the night," Penny said to Nancy, as they walked down Elm Street.

"So'm I," said Nancy. "No homework to do tonight. Maybe we can play a game or something."

"Rummy," said Penny. "Aunt Ivory likes rummy. And you can see the new trick she taught the cats."

"Another trick!" exclaimed Nancy. "Those cats can do about a dozen tricks already."

"I know," said Penny. Each night after supper, before she started working on next fall's quilt, Aunt Ivory put her cats through their tricks. The one where the cats stood in a circle with their paws on each other's backs. The one where James sat on Daniel's back while he walked in a figure eight on the braided rug. The one where all of them lay down in a row, and when Aunt Ivory snapped her fingers, rolled over all at once. And now the new one. Incredibly, in a week, Aunt Ivory had taught them to walk around the braided rug, all at once.

"Aunt Ivory's wonderful with animals," Penny said. "As soon as Tiger Boy is well enough, she's going to teach him some tricks too." Tiger Boy was the name she had given to the cat she had found in the graveyard.

But they never got to the rummy game. Aunt Ivory had just finished showing Nancy the new trick when there was an urgent knock at the door. It was Gramp. He walked in almost before he had finished knocking.

"I don't want to frighten you, Ivory," he said. "But Rusty Hanna came into the drugstore just now while I was down there, and he's drunk as a lord. Ranting and raging around about some cat of his that he says you have. Says he's going to get him if he has to tear your house down. Ugly as sin he was. Some of the boys are talking to him now trying to stop him. But," said Gramp, "in case they don't, you need a man in the house tonight. Probably he won't even show up, but I'm staying the night anyhow."

"Don't worry about us, Gramp," protested Aunt Ivory. "I can handle the situation." And Penny knew she could, after the ease with which she had got rid of Rusty Hanna the last time. But Gramp insisted that he was staying.

"Can't you let yourself get taken care of just *once*?" he asked. "I'd feel a lot better about it if you'd let me stay."

Aunt Ivory was about to give in when the kitchen door burst open. It was Hiram Crimmins. His face was red, and he was breathing hard from running.

"Has he been here?" he asked, when he had recovered enough wind to talk.

Gramp shook his head.

"Got away from us," Hiram sputtered. "Slipped away from us at the door of the bowling alley. Thought if we could get him in there, he'd stay. Last we saw he was heading this way."

No sooner had he finished speaking than the door flew open again and just as quickly closed behind Mr. Coffin, the undertaker. His face was very white and he could hardly speak. "He was hiding in the hedge by the cemetery," he panted. "We thought we had him, but he has a gun."

He didn't get any further. The door flew open once more, and Rusty Hanna lurched sideways through the door. By the light from the kitchen Penny saw the men who had followed Rusty up the hill. They were lined up against the cedar hedge, their hands in the air, and Rusty had his gun trained on them.

"—And keep them up," Rusty snarled. "The first man who makes a move will have a bullet through his gizzard." Rusty kept his gun aimed at the men as he turned his evil face toward the people in the kitchen. His pale eyes traveled from one face to the other.

"Where is she?" he demanded. "Where's

Ivory Perry?" Penny looked around the kitchen. At Nancy and Gramp. At Hiram Crimmins. At Mr. Coffin. Aunt Ivory wasn't there. She had slipped out when no one was looking.

Rusty turned on Penny. "You're the girl who stole my cat," he snapped. "You've got him hidden behind the stove. Go get him and bring him here."

Penny went behind the stove hardly realizing that she did so. It was as though she was forced to do it by the hard stare of the man's little eyes. She reached down and lifted up Tiger Boy. The wound on his back was still red and sore. Penny carried the cat over to Rusty Hanna. He grabbed Tiger Boy with his free hand and the cat mewed feebly for Rusty's grip pulled at the skin around the cut.

"Shut up," Rusty snarled at the cat. "And get back there," he said, pushing Penny back into the center of the room with his elbow. "That's all I'll be wanting tonight." He smiled evilly, his loose lips parted over his crooked yellow teeth. "I guess you won't be stealing many cats from now on. As for them—" he added, nodding his head at the men lined up against the cedar hedge.

"Drop that gun and drop that cat," came a level voice from the door that opened into the parlor. It was Aunt Ivory. She stood straight and severe between the plum velvet curtains in the doorway. In her hand she held a shiny, sinister-looking revolver. The smile faded off Rusty's face and he never finished what he was going to say. He didn't move in his amazement.

"I said drop that gun and drop that cat," Aunt Ivory repeated. The gun clattered to the floor and the cat dropped softly on his four feet. "Put Tiger Boy back behind the stove, Pam," Aunt Ivory said.

Penny went to do as she was told. But Rusty Hanna wasn't so drunk that he didn't know what he was doing. The second that Penny stood between him and the gun in Aunt Ivory's hand—the second that Aunt Ivory

would not have dared fire for fear of hitting Penny—before anyone realized what he was doing, Rusty Hanna made a dash for it and slammed the door behind him. They could hear him running down the steps and along the graveled walk. Hiram Crimmins threw open the door.

"After him!" he shouted to the men outside. But there was no need for shouting. The men were running pell-mell down the path already. Penny stood with the rest of them on the kitchen porch listening to the sound of running feet and shouts and branches being broken. Fifteen minutes later the men returned. They were upset and out of breath.

"Did he get away again?" Hiram asked.

"Yup," they said. "Like a greased eel in them bushes."

"We'll get him in the morning," said Hiram. But he was disappointed.

"I'll stay the night with Ivory and the girls," Gramp said. His deep laugh rumbled up from his stomach. "I dare say he won't be back for his tomcat tonight when he has a hellcat like Ivory to contend with first."

The men laughed in appreciation. Aunt Ivory blushed and smiled. It tickled Nancy and Penny to see how pleased she was to be called a "hellcat." Aunt Ivory, the minister's daughter!

"One thing, Ivory, just off the record. I don't remember you filing an application for a gun permit," Hiram said. Hiram Crimmins was town clerk as well as farmer. Aunt Ivory's smile stretched from ear to ear. "I didn't know you had to get a permit for a water pistol," she said.

CHAPTER EIGHT

Twidboro Becomes Unsafe

"YOU'VE GOT TO get out of town, Ivory," said Hiram Crimmins. He had come in the kitchen door of 11 Elm Street the next morning as Penny and Nancy and Gramp and Aunt Ivory were just sitting down to breakfast.

"Nonsense," said Aunt Ivory. "Pam and I can look after ourselves. Sit down and have some mackerel and coffee, Hiram," she said, getting him a plate.

"I can't force you to leave," said Hiram, stabbing his fish with a fork. "But I should hate to be responsible if anything happened to either of you. I looked it up in the records before I went home last night, and Rusty Hanna has taken out three gun permits. When the men went up to arrest him this morning he wasn't there. And neither were his guns. He had gone home too, for there was a half-empty pot of hot coffee on the stove. It would take a load off my mind if you'd just go away until we've rounded him up."

"Fiddlesticks," said Aunt Ivory. Then she added, "Besides, where could we go?"

"You must have relatives you could stay with," said Hiram.

Aunt Ivory shook her head.

"I have relatives," said Penny suddenly.

Aunt Ivory's face turned pale. "You don't know them, Pamela," she said.

"But I do," Penny insisted. "I met my twin at the fair, and—"

"And what?" Aunt Ivory asked. "Go on, Pamela."

Penny hesitated. Nancy kicked her under the table. "I'm going to tell," Penny said, looking at Nancy. But she didn't tell how she had switched places with Pam. All that at once would have been too much for Aunt Ivory. "Last Saturday," Penny continued, "we went down to Abbidydumkeag."

"I thought you said you went to Hatchet Cove." Aunt Ivory's voice was sharp. Above everything she hated lying. Penny's face grew red. She didn't know that they were meant to have gone to Hatchet Cove.

"We did, Ivory," said Gramp helpfully. "And after that we went to Abbidydumkeag."

"And I met my twin again," Penny went on.

"Did you meet—your father?" Aunt Ivory asked.

"Yes," said Penny. "Though I've only met him once, I think he's wonderful," she said soberly, putting in a plug for Barnabas.

"Yes," said Aunt Ivory. "Yes, I suppose you do." No one spoke for a while. They were all a little embarrassed.

"This is all silly," said Aunt Ivory, breaking the silence as she rose to stack the dishes. She took the dishes to the sink. "If we stay anywhere but here," she said with her back to the room, "we'll stay at the Knox Hotel in Thomaston."

Penny's face fell. She had given away part of the secret for nothing.

Gramp cleared his throat and went over and stood beside Aunt Ivory. "Mebbe you don't have the right to keep Pam from seeing Barnabas and her sister," he said. He knew he was hurting Aunt Ivory, but if their plan was to work, now was the chance. "You could let Pam stay out on the island with her father and sister and you could stay at Carrie Vinal's boardinghouse in town." If once they could get Aunt Ivory as far as Abbidydumkeag, the battle would be half won.

"We'll see," said Aunt Ivory. But they could tell by the tone of her voice that she was beaten. "At any rate, I can't leave the dishes dirty, Rusty Hanna or no Rusty Hanna."

Penny and Nancy grinned at each other, and

Hiram Crimmins said if everything was taken care of, well, he guessed he'd be going. Penny and Nancy were still grinning at each other when Aunt Ivory went upstairs and came down again with a Sears-Roebuck box under her arm.

"As long as you're going visiting," she said giving the box to Penny, "you might as well wear something decent." Penny tore off the wrappings. Inside, carefully done up in tissue paper, was the red plaid dress with the round white collar from page 157 in the Sears-Roebuck fall and winter catalogue. She had secretly been eyeing it ever since the catalogue came to Indian Island, though she would never have admitted it to her father or Barney. They would have laughed because she had always scorned dresses. And here it was! But it wasn't hers. It was Pam's.

"Oh, Aunt Ivory," she said, "it's beautiful!"

"Glad you like it," said Aunt Ivory brusquely, though secretly she was pleased that Penny was so delighted. "Go upstairs and put it on."

Penny did as she was told, but she didn't want to because the dress was Pam's and it was new.

When Aunt Ivory and Penny had packed their nightgowns and a clean change of clothes they started off in the truck with Gramp. They stopped at the Drakes' to leave Nancy and the five white cats and to pick up Gramp's toothbrush, for he said he would stay overnight at Abbidydumkeag. Penny held Tiger Boy in her arms. They had decided to give him to the twin on Indian Island lest there be any further trouble with Rusty Hanna or his yellow dog.

"I hope Penelope will like cats as well as you do, Pam," said Aunt Ivory, as they bounced along the river road. It was a gray day but the clouds were high and the air was clear. The fields were brown and the Camden hills in the distance were blue and sharply distinct. The trees were nearly all bare now, save a few sturdy oaks which stubbornly hung on to their brown and rattling leaves. For it was October

28th already. Occasionally they passed a farm with a gay pile of orange pumpkins and yellow squashes beside a gray and weather-beaten barn. They had started late and it was dinner-time when they reached Abbidydumkeag.

"Do you think they'll have enough extra food for three of us?" Penny asked.

"Two," corrected Aunt Ivory. "I'm eating at Carrie Vinal's."

"Aw, Ivory—" began Gramp.

"Don't say anything more," interrupted Aunt Ivory. "You got me this far against my will. And you're not going to get me any further than Carrie's boardinghouse."

"All right, Ivory," said Gramp. "Don't get het up about it." And he drove the truck up to Mrs. Vinal's boardinghouse. He and Penny got out with Aunt Ivory and carried her suitcase into the house. There was nothing to distinguish it from the other white houses on the road except that it was a great deal larger, and it boasted a veranda that ran along the front of the house facing the harbor. It was too cold for sitting on the porch now, and a row of white rockers were standing backward with their backs leaning against the wall and their rungs in the air. They walked up the steps and knocked on the door. It was Mrs. Vinal who came to the door, and Penny would have greeted her with glee until she remembered that she was Pamela and would continue to be Pamela for another hour or so. She felt silly standing there in the new red plaid dress and acting as though she had never seen the jolly, fat Mrs. Vinal before.

"Land sakes!" exclaimed Mrs. Vinal. "If it ain't Ivory Perry. And not looking a day over eighteen neither. I never thought I'd see you down here. What brung you anyhow?"

Aunt Ivory blushed and would have explained, but Mrs. Vinal hadn't stopped talking yet. Mrs. Vinal turned to Gramp who was beaming roguishly at her.

"Might have known it would be old Cupid who brung you down!" she cried. Mrs. Vinal and Gramp had gone to school together. Even in those days he had been fat and pink like a cherub. Gramp frowned and looked at Aunt Ivory. He hoped she hadn't heard his old nickname, for she might become suspicious that there was some matchmaking going on. Evidently she hadn't, and Mrs. Vinal didn't mention it again, for now she had turned to Penny.

"This Barnabas's girl?" she asked. "Except for the clothes and the haircut, she's the spitting image of Penny."

Penny grinned.

"I'm going to take Pam out to Indian Island now," said Gramp. "Ivory thought mebbe she could stay here with you."

Mrs. Vinal looked puzzled. It seemed Ivory Perry hadn't come to see Barnabas after all. Gramp noticed her look of bewilderment.

"Ivory'll tell you all about it," he said. Then he took Mrs. Vinal aside. Penny couldn't hear all of what they were saying. They were talking in whispers. Mrs. Vinal nodded her head once or twice. Penny heard her call Gramp an "old rogue." And Gramp said, "I'll be there too." And then Mrs. Vinal said, "You old rogue," more emphatically. And her cheeks were pinker than ever. If that were possible.

"We can go home tonight if they catch him, can't we?" Aunt Ivory asked Gramp, when the whispered conversation was over.

"Of course, Ivory, of course," said Gramp. "Come on, Pam. We don't want to miss out on any food." Penny and Gramp went down the steps leaving Aunt Ivory in the jolly company of Mrs. Vinal.

"See you later," Mrs. Vinal called.

Gramp grinned. Penny couldn't see why he was so gleeful. Here they had got Aunt Ivory all the way to Abbidydumkeag, and not only had she refused to go out to Indian Island, but she wanted to go home tonight if it were possible. Penny said as much to Gramp as she followed him down the hill to the wharves with the cat in her arms.

"Don't worry, Pam," Gramp said. "I'm not such a foolish old codger as you think."

"But what are you going to do, Gramp? How are you going to get Aunt Ivory out to Indian Island?"

"Did you ever hear the story about Mohammed and the mountain?" Gramp asked.

Penny shook her head no. By this time they were at the wharf. They saw Floyd down at the end dropping green lobsters into the lobster car.

"Back again?" Floyd called. "Row you out, if you want." Gramp accepted his offer. All the way out, Penny teased him to tell her the story about Mohammed and the mountain. Gramp didn't say a word. He just smiled exasperatingly.

"Please," begged Penny. "And I'll never ask you another thing as long as I live."

But Gramp maintained his silence to the bitter end. It wasn't till they got to the door of the stone house that he said anything. And what he said was just as cryptic as his other answers.

"What day is it, Pam?" he asked.

"Saturday," answered Penny.

"That's the answer to your questions," said Gramp. "And don't say anything about your aunt Ivory being in town in front of your father."

Before Penny could coax any more answers out of him, the door flew open and there was Pam in Penny's overalls. Behind her were Barney and Barnabas.

"We saw you coming from the window," they said in chorus.

"Cat and all," added Barney.

Needless to say, there was a great deal of commotion and excitement which continued until at length the meal was over.

"Whew, that was a good meal," Gramp said at last. He wiped his mouth on the back of his hand and widened his already wide belt.

"Penny's been outdoing herself this past week with her cooking," Barnabas said proudly, and Pam grinned. It was lucky for her that Aunt

Ivory had insisted on her learning to cook.

"Whee," said Penny, rising from the table and patting her bulging stomach, "I'm going to get into some overalls."

"Wonder what Ivory would say, Pam, if she could see that unladylike gesture," remarked Gramp with a hearty laugh.

"Acts as if she owned the house already," said Barnabas indulgently, "and all the overalls in it."

Penny realized then that she was still meant to be Pam in a red plaid dress.

"Can I borrow a pair, Penny?" asked Penny.

Pam nodded her head in assent. She was shaking so with laughter that she could not speak. And the two girls went up the rope ladder and through the hatch.

"Jimminy!" shrieked Penny when she saw her room. Barnabas had been busy with his saw and hammer while Penny was away. Instead of one bunk under the window, there were now two. An upper berth and a lower. The top bunk began at the halfway point of the window so that whoever slept in the upper could also look out and see across Penobscot Bay in the morning.

"Puppa built that so that you could come and spend the night with me. I mean, so that I could come and spend the night with you. What I mean is that whoever is Pam can come and spend the night with whoever is Penny." Pam said this all in one breath and the result was a little confusing. But Penny understood perfectly. She noticed that Pam found no difficulty now in saying "Puppa."

"Maybe you can spend the night tonight," said Penny. "You mean," said Pam, "you mean, the Period of Trial is up?"

Penny saw Pam's face fall. "You like it here," she cried. And she seized Pam around the waist and danced her about the room.

"I love it," said Pam sadly. Though it was hard to sound sad while she was being spun around the room by Penny. "But I thought we had decided to do it for two weeks," she panted. "Didn't you like Aunt Ivory enough to stay longer?"

"Aunt Ivory is over in the village at Mrs. Vinal's boardinghouse," Penny gasped, as she fell exhausted on the lower bunk.

"Aunt Ivory!" Pam's face was white. "How did she find out?"

"She didn't find out," said Penny. "All she knows is that Gramp brought you and Nancy down here last Saturday. That's all."

"But what's she doing in Abbidydumkeag?"

Penny told Pam about Rusty Hanna and the cat and how Aunt Ivory had scared him away with a water pistol.

"She sure is wonderful," Penny said at the end.

"Oh, I'm glad you like her," Pam said. The Period of Trial had certainly been a success. "But now what are we going to do? That's going to be the hardest part."

"That's what I asked Gramp," Penny

replied. "We got her as far as Abbidydumkeag, but wild horses couldn't drag her out to Indian Island."

"What did Gramp say?" asked Pam.

"He asked me whether I had ever heard the story about Mohammed and the mountain. But that just doesn't make sense."

"Yes, it does," said Pam excitedly. "Mohammed wouldn't come to the mountain so the mountain had to go to Mohammed. Aunt Ivory won't come to Indian Island so Indian Island has to go to Aunt Ivory."

"That still doesn't make sense," Penny scoffed. "How can Indian Island go to Aunt Ivory? I still think Gramp is crazy. Just before we got to the door he asked me what day it was, and when I said 'Saturday' he said that was the answer to all my questions. Now if that makes sense—"

"Don't you see," Pam interrupted, "he doesn't mean Indian Island is the mountain. He means Puppa is."

"But what did he mean about Saturday?"

"Well, isn't Saturday night a special night here, too?"

"Of course!" shouted Penny. "Everyone goes into town on Saturday night. We always do. Puppa and Barney and I. And there's a dance every Saturday night at the Grange. Do you think that could be it?"

"I think maybe it could," said Pam.

CHAPTER NINE

The Mountain Comes to Mohammed

PENNY SWUNG herself down from the last rung of the rope ladder. Pam followed her as expertly as one monkey follows another. She had learned a lot in a week's time. She could maneuver the dory into the cleft in the rocks; she knew who owned which lobster pots, which lobsters were by law too small to be kept and must be thrown back into the water, and many other things. All these Barney had taught her. But he couldn't help her with her schoolwork, for he was only in third grade. That had been the only black spot in her visit to Indian Island. She had done very well in Arithmetic and Miss Baker, the teacher, had praised her warmly—adding,

"I knew if you put your mind to it, Penelope, you could be a good math student." But in Spelling Pam had failed miserably. Each day she had had to stay after school and go over the day's lesson with her teacher. And still she could not tell the difference between "stationary" and "stationery." Nor between "council" and "counsel." Miss Baker was dumbfounded, for Penny stood at the top of her class in Spelling. Even though that part of the visit had been unpleasant, Pam felt very blue about having to leave Indian Island. Penny was looking sad, too, at supper for she didn't want Pam to go, either.

"Cheer up, you two," Barnabas had said to the two girls in blue overalls. "Gramp says he'll arrange it so that Pam can stay the night. The old Romeo wants to go to the dance tonight at the Grange. So I said we'd all go. That is," he said, winking at Gramp, "if we don't cramp his style."

"Don't worry about my style," laughed

Gramp. And that settled it.

"You girls hop upstairs and get dolled up," Barnabas said. "I want to be proud of you tonight."

"Oh dear!" said Penny when they got upstairs. "Puppa will be much prouder of you than he will be of me. I haven't got anything to wear but overalls." She looked at the red plaid dress lying neatly across the back of a chair. It was Pam's dress now.

"Why don't you look in the closet?" asked Pam. "I washed and ironed all your overalls and blouses."

"Overalls!" thought Penny. It was all right going to the Grange in overalls when you were eleven, but at twelve you ought to have a dress.

Penny went over to the closet and opened the door. There hanging neatly on a hanger beside the white blouses was another red plaid dress just like the one she had worn that morning! She squealed with delight.

"Puppa thought you ought to have a dress

now that you are twelve," Pam said. "I helped him pick it out. I hope you like it."

"It's the very one I would have picked," cried Penny.

"Better not thank him because I've already done that for you," said Pam.

"And I've already thanked Aunt Ivory for yours."

The two girls scrambled into the red plaid dresses and swung themselves down the rope ladder, alike as two peas in a pod.

"Boy! you look nice," said Barney, when they came into the kitchen. Compliments of this nature were rare from Barney.

"It's a conspiracy!" whooped Gramp. "First it's overalls and now it's dresses."

Barnabas didn't say anything but he was smiling proudly. He was still smiling proudly when they got to the Grange. The night was quiet and filled with moonlight. All the way in in the dory they had heard the music across the water. And the sound of people laughing. As they climbed the hill to the Grange Hall, the music grew louder. The orchestra was playing "Put on Your Old Gray Bonnet" and "Oh, Dem Golden Slippers" and "Turkey in the Straw"—all the tunes that Pam and Penny knew—one right after the other and very fast.

"Oh, shucks," said Gramp. "It's a Lady of the Lake. Best dance going. I sure hate to miss one."

Then the orchestra broke into the "Arkansas Traveler" and the tempo increased. The fiddle was going as fast as it could. *"Everyone spin!"* shouted someone. It was the end of the dance. As Gramp and Barnabas and the children came up out of the night into the light streaming through the doorway of the Grange Hall, the music stopped, and the couples were going back to their seats on the benches that ran around the walls of the room. The men who had been dancing, had their coats off and now were wiping their faces with handkerchiefs. With flushed faces, the women sank exhausted on the welcome benches. Barnabas had Penny and Pam each by the hand. He smiled proudly to all his friends as he led them to a vacant place on the benches. The friends smiled back. But there were some who eyed him curiously. The news had got about that Ivory Perry was in town, and the more inquisitive of the townspeople were wondering what would come of it. For they knew she would have nothing to do with Barnabas Kellyhorn.

"Only decent that she should let the girl see her father now and again," Pam heard the woman next to her on the bench whisper to a friend.

"Don't mind her," Penny whispered to Pam. "That's only mean old Ermina Mink. She's an awful gossip."

"I had forgotten it was the Hallow'een dance tonight," said Barney excitedly. "So many other things were happening."

They looked with large pleased eyes around the gayly decorated Grange Hall. In the corners of the room, and banking the stage where the orchestra sat, were stacks of cornstalks fastened together with orange and black crepe-paper streamers. At the foot of them were piles of orange squashes and pumpkins and red and yellow ears of corn. On top of the dark, old upright piano sat a jack-o'-lantern with a hideous grin slashed in his face. And all along the sills of the tall windows on either side of the long room sat other jack-o'-lanterns, some grinning, some frowning. Others had big round surprised eyes and one was winking. Twisted streamers of black and orange crepe paper crossed and recrossed each other above their heads. They had barely time to take it all in before the electric lights in the room went out. The only light there was came from the dozens of jack-o'-lanterns along the windowsills.

"It's a waltz," predicted Gramp. He knew all the customs of the country dance halls as well as every figure of even the most complicated dances. He was right. The orchestra started playing "Carolina Moon" and the fiddler and his fiddle swayed dreamily in a very slow three-quarter time. Barney leaped from his seat and grabbed Pam by the hand.

"C'mon," he said.

"Shall I, or do you want to?" Barnabas asked, leaning across Penny to Gramp.

"You go ahead," said Gramp gallantly. "I'll sit this one out." He was eyeing the door where some people were just coming in. Penny jumped up and started waltzing with her father. He was a very good dancer. He spun Penny around in big sweeping circles and her full, red skirt billowed out behind. Dancing with him was a far different matter from dancing with Barney, she thought, as they circled past Barney and Pam.

Pam was having her difficulties. They had only gone a few steps when Barney said, "I don't even have to hunt for the freckles on your nose to know you're not Penny."

"Why not?" asked Pam.

"Because Penny always makes me count when I dance with her," he said, breathing hard.

"Well, maybe you ought," said Pam. For Barney plodded along without listening to the music.

"Heck!" grunted Barney, taking another huge step and planting his heavy shoe on her toe. "One, two, three," he said loudly. "One, two, three. Step, close, step. One, two, three." They had gone all the way around the room and now they were back where they had started. Pam turned to smile at Gramp. But Gramp had disappeared.

"Look," said Barney. "There's Gramp. With Mrs. Vinal!" He forgot all about counting and pushed Pam along with big strides trying to catch up with the twirling Widow Vinal. But Gramp, for all his age and weight, was an even speedier dancer than Barney. It wasn't till the waltz ended and the lights came up that they were standing side by side at the foot of the stage. Gramp kicked at a red ear of corn that was sprawling out on the dance floor.

"Wish it was a corn husking, Carrie," he said, giving Mrs. Vinal's plump waist a squeeze before he let go of her. Barney poked Pam in the ribs. He knew that at a corn husking whoever found a red ear could kiss whomever he pleased—if he could catch her.

"Go 'long with you, Cupid," cried Mrs. Vinal, giving Gramp a push. "Hello, there," she cried, spying Pam and Barney. "Don't the hall look pretty, though?"

"It sure does," they said, nodding their heads.

"Be right with you," said Gramp, taking Mrs. Vinal back to her seat across the room.

"Who's that pretty lady in the red dress next to Mrs. Vinal?" Barney asked, as he and Pam went back to their seats. Pam looked across the hall.

"Why, it's Aunt Ivory," Pam said. She had never seen Aunt Ivory looking so pretty before. Perhaps it was the dress. It was just like the ones that she and Penny were wearing except that it was a grown-up one.

"Where's Gramp?" Barnabas asked them, when they got back to their seats.

"Over there with Mrs. Vinal," said Barney, pointing. Pam held her breath as she watched Barnabas look across the floor.

"Who's that pretty woman next to her?" he asked. Then the color left his face. "Why," he said, "why, it's Ivory Perry! But what is she doing here? Tell me—" he said, turning to Pam and Penny, "whichever one of you is Pam—tell me whatever brought her here? She wouldn't have come of her own free will!"

The twins between them blurted out the story of Rusty Hanna and the cat.

"Why, the little hellcat," he said admiringly. Then he added, "But whatever brought her to the Grange? She knows I love to dance. She must have known I'd be here." They looked over at Aunt Ivory. She hadn't seen them. She was talking and laughing with Mrs. Vinal and Gramp.

"I think probably Gramp and Mrs. Vinal had something to do with it," suggested Penny.

"Why, the old rascals," said Barnabas. But he didn't seem to mind at all. Pam and Penny and Barney sighed with relief. They watched Gramp walk down the hall to the stage. The fiddler leaned down to Gramp's level with his fiddle under his arm. Gramp asked him something. The fiddler nodded his head and turned and spoke to the woman at the piano and the man with the accordion. And the orchestra broke into the first few bars of the "Arkansas Traveler." Gramp had requested another Lady of the Lake.

"I'd like to ask your aunt Ivory to dance with me," said Barnabas, "but I don't think she would."

"Get your partners for the Lady of the Lake," shouted the fiddler.

"She's dancing with Gramp, anyhow," said Barney. "So she couldn't dance with you."

"Dance with me instead, Puppa," pleaded

Penny. She dragged her father out onto the floor. Pam sat with Barney and watched the ladies line up on one side of the room and the men on the other.

"First and every other couple cross over," shouted the fiddler. Aunt Ivory crossed over but Penny didn't.

"That means that Puppa will have to spin Aunt Ivory when she gets to him," Barney said excitedly. "I bet Gramp fixed that."

"Every gentleman spin the lady on his left," called the fiddler, taking up his bow. And the Lady of the Lake had begun.

"Look at Aunt Ivory!" cried Pam.

Aunt Ivory was in the center now, spinning with Gramp. Her red dress was flying and her cheeks were very pink. "I didn't know she could dance like that."

"Christmas! she's good," said Barney with awe. "She's the best dancer in the room." And she was. She could do the Lady of the Lake better than any of them. In and out she went.

Spinning on the side, spinning in the center, weaving in and out of the other dancers, all the time working up the room. And all the time Barnabas was working down the room. Until finally they were only one couple away. Pam clutched Barney's sleeve.

"Look," she said, "she's dancing with Puppa."

Aunt Ivory danced into the arms of Barnabas without realizing who was to spin her next. And then she looked into his face. Her pink cheeks grew white.

"Evening, Ivory," Pam and Barney heard Barnabas say.

"Good evening, Barnabas," Aunt Ivory said. And all the time they were spinning wildly. Aunt Ivory turned her head away as though she didn't want to speak any longer.

"You look mighty pretty in that dress," said Barnabas. "You always did look well in red."

Aunt Ivory didn't say anything, but her cheeks grew pink again.

"May I have the next dance?" Barnabas asked boldly. But Aunt Ivory didn't have time to answer, for it was time to spin in the center with Gramp.

"She didn't say 'no,' anyhow," Barney said excitedly as the Lady of the Lake came to a finish in a final, frantic burst of spinning. Barnabas took advantage of this fact and when the next dance commenced he went straight across the room to Aunt Ivory and bobbed his head. Ermina Mink nudged her neighbor. Everyone was waiting to see what Ivory Perry would do. Perhaps because they were, Aunt Ivory did what she did. She stood up and gave her hand to Barnabas. The twins sat close together on the bench hardly daring to breathe as they watched. Their brown eyes never left Barnabas as they twirled about the room. For a long time Barnabas did all the talking and Aunt Ivory just nodded once or twice. Then she nodded more frequently and began to talk. When the dance ended she was even smiling as Barnabas brought her not to the side of the room where she had been sitting but back to where Penny and Pam and Barney were.

"Just for the looks of things, Ivory," they heard Barnabas say. And Aunt Ivory laughed. After that Barnabas and Aunt Ivory danced every dance together. Penny and Pam were beside themselves. They could hardly believe it. Gramp and Mrs. Vinal were beaming like a couple of successful rogues as they bounced happily around the room. The dance ended long before they wanted it to.

"Good night!" everyone was calling as the orchestra began putting their instruments away.

"We'll see you home," said Gramp, tucking his arm under Mrs. Vinal's as they went out the door.

Barnabas took Aunt Ivory's arm. "Just for the looks of things," he said again. "We can't have all the women of Abbidydumkeag saying we're just a couple of soreheads." But Penny and Pam and Barney noticed that he didn't remove his arm when they had left the light of the Grange Hall behind them. Nor did Aunt Ivory pull hers away from him until they were back at Mrs. Vinal's boardinghouse. And then it was only to say good night.

CHAPTER TEN

The Note

"I'M A LIAR AND a cheat," said Gramp from his seat in the stern of the dory. They were rowing in to church through the choppy, gray waves. "I telephoned home during intermission last night, and when Nancy told me that they had caught Rusty Hanna yesterday afternoon in the bushes behind the graveyard, I went back and told Ivory that he was still at large. Because I had promised her I would take her home as soon as he was caught." The old sinner tossed his white curls and chuckled.

Barnabas laughed, too, looking up from his oars. "If anyone had told me yesterday that Ivory Perry was going to be at the dance last night, wild horses couldn't have dragged me there. But when I saw her there looking just like Penny's and Pam's older sister—well, things were different." He pulled the boat in to the wharf whistling "The Old Gray Mare." And they climbed the hill to Carrie Vinal's boardinghouse all singing:

"The old gray mare,
she ain't what she used to be,
Ain't what she used to be,
ain't what she used to be.
The old gray mare,
she ain't what she used to be,
Many long years ago."

The door flew open as they climbed the porch steps and there stood Mrs. Vinal in a purple Sunday hat and gloves. She had heard them coming. In fact, all of Abbidydumkeag must have heard their lusty singing. And she was ready to go with them to church.

"Where's Ivory?" asked Barnabas.

Mrs. Vinal's smile of welcome left her face. "She's gone," she said. "She left right after breakfast on the stage." The stage was an old station wagon that made one round trip a day from Abbidydumkeag, through Hatchet Cove, and up the river road to Twidboro.

"But, Carrie," Gramp protested, "you promised me you wouldn't tell Ivory that Rusty was caught."

"I didn't," Mrs. Vinal said. "The boy that brings the milk was the one who upset the applecart. The first thing he said this morning was, 'Did y'hear tell about Rusty Hanna up to Twidboro? Put him in jail yesterday afternoon for disturbing the peace.' What could I do?"

"Did she blow up?" asked Gramp.

"No. She was very quiet. She just said, 'That settles it.' And she packed her bag and left on the stage. I couldn't stop her."

"But what about me?" asked Pam.

"For land sakes, I clear forgot. Here's a note

she left you." Mrs. Vinal opened her pocketbook and pulled out an envelope. "You're sure you're Pam?" she queried, looking at Pam and Penny in their red plaid dresses.

"Yes, I'm sure," said Pam, taking the envelope. She tore it open and read the note.

Dear Pamela [it said],
"When I saw you and Penelope in your red dresses last night, I realized that you and she belonged together. You both seemed so happy. And your father was so proud of you that I haven't the heart to ask you to come back to the drab spinster existence of 11 Elm Street. Therefore, today, the twenty-ninth of October, I am turning you over to your father. I am going to ask you not to try to see me again. It is very hard for me to do this, but it would be still harder and very awkward for all of us if I were constantly seeing your father. For I still feel the same way about him as I did before he married your mother. I realized last night that Gramp and Mrs. Vinal were encouraging this sentiment, but I did not

want to make a fuss for fear the towns-people would talk. ["My eye," said Gramp when he read this.] And I am sure they did this only in order to bring you and Penelope together. Therefore, they can consider that their efforts have been rewarded, and I shall quietly drop out of the picture. You have your cat and I shall send the rest of your belongings back with the stage this afternoon. Do not follow me. I will not be there. I am going away. There is something that I have always wanted to do. And I am going to do it now. My best to your new family, and may you have a happy life on Indian Island.

Lovingly,
Aunt Ivory

Pam silently handed the letter to the others.

"Women!" spluttered Gramp, when he had finished. "Women and hens! They're always running away. Someone ought to teach them that there's such a thing as running too much."

"In a way I don't blame her," said Mrs.

Vinal. "Women like to do their own matchmaking. We should have known better."

"If we hadn't done anything," said Gramp, trying to reassure himself, "Penny and Pam would never have known each other."

"Yes," said Barnabas, "and Ivory would never have left home. She's such a little piece to be traipsing around by herself."

"I guess she can take care of herself," said Gramp, remembering Rusty Hanna and the water pistol.

"Besides," added Mrs. Vinal, "she says she's going to do something she's always wanted to do."

"Still," said Barnabas, "I don't like it."

"I don't either," said Mrs. Vinal.

"Neither do I," added Pam. "I'm going back this afternoon with Gramp."

"But she won't be there," said Penny. They had worked so hard on their plan, and now that half of it was about to come true Pam was not going to go through with it.

"She can't have left so quickly," said Pam with tears in her eyes. She hadn't realized when she and Nancy had first talked about Penny that rainy day in the Hen House, that she wouldn't give up Aunt Ivory for anything in the world. Not even a wonderful twin like Penny. "I've got to go back," she said.

"Yes, I suppose you do," said Barnabas with an effort. Now that he had found his daughter he didn't want to give her up. "And I'm coming with you. If we get there in time to stop her from leaving," he said hopefully, "maybe there will be a wedding at 11 Elm Street next June."

"We can go right now," said Gramp, thinking of the prospect of a June wedding. "I guess it won't hurt to miss church just this one Sunday."

That settled it. Without even bothering to row out to Indian Island for Pam's nightgown or Gramp's toothbrush (for Gramp had slept in half of Barnabas's big bed the night before—only it was closer to three-quarters) they started up the river road to Twidboro. Mrs. Vinal and Penny and Barney walked to church in a much less cheerful fashion than they had walked home from the Grange the night before.

"I wonder what it can be that Aunt Ivory intends to do?" Barney asked the others. But none of them knew the answer.

Pam asked Barnabas and Gramp the same question as they bounced along the dirt road. But they only shook their heads. Neither of them had known that Ivory Perry cherished other ideas in her head besides making quilts and taking care of Pam and the cats.

"Maybe we can stop her from doing whatever it is," they said. But they never found out what it was because when they got to the little white house on Elm Street, Aunt Ivory wasn't there. Even before they saw the padlocks on the doors and found the windows locked, they knew she wouldn't be home. No smoke came from the skinny, brick chimney and a pile of pasteboard boxes sat on the front steps. A note on top of them said, *For Pamela Kellyhorn. Please deliver to Carrie Vinal's boardinghouse.* That was all.

"What about the cats?" asked Pam. Her chin looked like a peachstone, but she didn't cry.

"Yes, the cats," Gramp agreed. "We ought to do something about them."

They got in the truck and went up the street to the square, yellow, hip-roofed house that was the Drakes'. Nancy was out in back vigorously raking leaves. Some black hens were pecking and stuffing their craws in front of the stable. But there wasn't a cat in sight.

"Did you have a good time?" Nancy called.

"Where are Ivory Perry's cats?" Gramp asked without answering her question.

"Why? Aren't they at home?" Nancy leaned her rake against the stable and came over to them.

"No," Pam said. "And neither is Aunt Ivory."

"That's funny," said Nancy. "She came and got them just before church. She had on her black Sunday dress with the white ruffle. I figured that she was going to take them home and feed them before she went to church."

"Did you see her in church?" Barnabas asked.

"No, I didn't," Nancy answered. "I looked for Pam, but I couldn't find her."

"I wasn't there," said Pam. "We just got home. Aunt Ivory came up on the stage."

"Was she alone when she came here, Nancy?" Gramp asked.

"No," said Nancy. "Hiram Crimmins was with her. He had his car out front, and they put the cats in some baskets and Hiram carried them out to the car."

"Come on," said Barnabas. "We've got to find Hiram."

"But what's it all about?" Nancy asked, running along beside them as they went back to the truck.

Pam explained on the way up to Hiram's farm. The truck with the two girls in the dump part rattled up Elm Street under the tunnel formed by the arching branches of the elm trees on either side of the street. Halfway up the hill, where Elm Street curved to the left to meet the river road again, a narrow road branched off into the dark silent woods on the right. Gramp turned into it and shifted the truck into second, for the road was nothing more than two wheel ruts, which wound over the pine needles and flat granite boulders up the hill through the spruce and pine trees. Now and again the loud flapping of wings meant that some fish hawk had been startled from its roosting place high in the trees by the rattling truck. The air was punctuated by the raucous calls of the big, black crows swaying in the singing crowns of the spruce trees.

On any other day Pam would have been eagerly listening to all the noises of the woods and breathing deeply the smell of pitch and pine needles. This was one of her favorite places. But not today. She hardly noticed the woods at all, for her eyes were on the road. After about half a mile the road came out into the open. They were approaching the brow of the hill now and the woods were behind them. No trees grew here save one or two tamaracks which, like the juniper and blueberry bushes, were thriving on the poor and rocky soil. Perched on top where the hill leveled off sat Hiram Crimmins's stand of buildings.

Across a small valley, on top of another bare hill, was Rusty Hanna's tattered house. But Hiram's house, though plain and unshuttered and a weather-beaten white, looked neat and in good repair. A long string of sheds stretched from the house to the red barn where Hiram kept his prize oxen. Two goats were busily cropping what they could of the stubbly, autumn grass as the truck drove up. Three cars were parked by the barn but there was no one about. One was Hiram's and the others must have belonged to Sunday company.

They did. For when Gramp and Barnabas and Penny and Nancy entered the house, they found, sitting in a buzz of conversation around a table laden with chicken and dumplings and turnips and mustard piccalilli, Hiram's wife's cousins from Waldoboro and Hiram's brother and his children from Port Clyde, as well as Hiram, his wife, and his two nearly grown sons. They all looked up from their plates as Gramp and Barnabas and the girls came in. The conversation stopped and hung in midair. Nobody said anything for a moment.

"Speak of angels and they flap their wings," said Mrs. Crimmins, coming to the rescue.

"Well, well," said Hiram. "We were just talking about you, Pam. Thought you were staying down to Abbidydumkeag for good."

"That's what we're here to find out about," said Barnabas. "Where did you take Ivory Perry?"

"To the station like she said," said Hiram. "She said she was going away for a while, and that Pam was going to live with her father from now on."

"Did she say where she was going?" asked Gramp.

"Heard her ask the stationmaster for a ticket to Boston. Said she'd get another ticket when she got there. She made some fuss because he said the cats would have to go in the baggage car until he said she could sit in there with them."

"Did you hear whether she asked for a round-trip ticket?" Pam asked. She was really crying now.

"I'm afraid I heard her say, 'One way, please,'" said Hiram gently, the way he did when he had to hurt a sick animal.

"When's the next train to Boston, Hiram?" asked Barnabas, his arm about Pam's shoulders. "I'm going after her."

"About three o'clock," said Hiram. "And good luck to the both of you."

So at five o'clock, a woebegone Pam sat on the front steps of Number 11 Elm Street beside the pasteboard boxes filled with her belongings. She was waiting for the stage which would carry her back to Abbidydumkeag and Indian Island and the home she had fought so to have. But she had not counted on having to leave Aunt Ivory—Aunt Ivory who was at this minute sitting in a baggage car in her Sunday dress bound for Boston with her five white cats. Hiram had said she was going still farther. But she had not told him where or why. Pam's chin trembled. But she didn't want to cry in front of Nancy again.

"Where do you suppose she's gone?" Pam asked, trying to make conversation until she had to say good-bye.

Nancy only shook her head. Her chin was trembling, too. Behind them the pointed windows of the little white house shone brightly as though they knew the answer to Pam's question.

PART II
WINTER

CHAPTER ELEVEN

Christmas Eve

IT WAS CHRISTMAS even in Twidboro. Though only four-thirty, dusk was quickly swallowing up all the traces of daylight. The streetlights were already on. And through the kitchen windows, behind the Christmas wreaths silhouetted against the lamplight, housewives could be seen preparing their five o'clock suppers. The stores were brightly shining and their windows were decorated with lights and tinsel. The windows of the drugstore were filled with piles of candy boxes reposing on wads of cotton batting snow. The Five and Ten was crowded with people making last-minute purchases of Christmas tree lights and tinsel and stars and ribbons and wrapping paper and candy canes. People stood in line before the toy counter. Crowded into the line were Pam and Penny. Somehow they had managed to break away from Barney and Barnabas who had clung like leeches all afternoon. Each time the twins thought they had got rid of the men, they had heard a patter of feet, and Barney would appear puffing and saying he thought he had lost them. Pam would give Penny a look of dismay, and then the girls would have to begin all over again trying to get off by themselves so that Barney and Barnabas would not see what they were buying. And now, finally, with only half an hour before the stage left, the twins had managed to sneak off by themselves to the Five and Ten. Pam already had one package under her arm from the counter on the other side of the room: a pair of red wool socks for Barnabas to wear under his big black rubber boots.

"That's what I'm going to get Puppa," said Penny, pointing to a round crystal globe sitting on a little stand. Inside it was a misshapen polar bear sitting on the top of an iceberg. Penny reached for it and turned it upside down before she set it down again. A small snowstorm gently settled on the head and shoulders of the bear and on the iceberg. Pam's eyes shone with envy.

"I wish I'd thought of that," she said wistfully. "But," she added, "I guess maybe he'll like the socks."

"I'll say," said Penny. "They're beautiful and furry, and besides they're red and that's his favorite color."

It was their turn now at the counter. "I'll take this," said Penny, handing the salesgirl the polar bear. While it was being wrapped they each picked out a present for Barney. Penny bought a scout knife with a big blade and a little blade, a corkscrew, and a nail file inside it. And Pam bought a game with little cardboard fishes with rings in their mouths and wooden fish poles with magnets on the ends of the lines.

Their final purchases were being wrapped up when they noticed Barney's red-tasseled cap over at the counter where the Christmas-tree lights were sold. In one hand he held a silver star with a red tinsel center. It was the most beautiful star they had ever seen.

"Barney!" Penny called, as they went over to him. "Are you going to buy that?"

"It's a surprise for Uncle Barnabas," Barney explained. "I want our tree to be the best tree there ever was."

"It certainly ought to be with that," said Pam. "Where's Puppa?"

"He's in the drugstore. He told me to come find you. I didn't think I'd ever get away so that I could buy this without him seeing me."

"Let's go," said Penny. "The stage leaves in fifteen minutes."

"Okay," said Barney, taking the package the salesgirl handed him. When they reached the sidewalk they found that a light snow was settling over the village. A snow as gentle and silent as the snowstorm inside the globe with the polar bear.

"We're going to have a white Christmas after all," said Penny happily. "This is the kind of snow that lasts all night."

When they reached the drugstore, they found Barnabas leaning against the counter chatting with Mr. Drake and Nancy, who was helping out. Lined up on the counter were four cups of hot chocolate with whipped cream heaped on top. "Nancy!" Pam shrieked. "I didn't think we were going to see you. We stopped at your house and your mother said you were out in the woods getting your tree with Gramp."

"We got a white pine this year," said Nancy. "And it's going to have nothing on it but tons of silver tinsel and blue lights."

"I wish I were going to see it," said Pam wistfully. In spite of all the happy evenings she had spent on Indian Island stringing popcorn and cranberries for the tree, and making chains and lanterns of colored paper, in spite of the fun of sending away to Sears-Roebuck for a cuckoo clock for Barnabas, and handkerchiefs embroidered with an *I* for Aunt Ivory, and fur-lined gloves for Penny, in spite of the excitement of climbing the spruce-clad knoll on Indian Island, and picking out their own tree with Penny and Barney and Barnabas, and cutting balsam boughs and ground pine, and making wreaths for every window in the house and in the lighthouse—in spite of all this, Christmas had a note of dreariness in it for Pamela Kellyhorn. Because Aunt Ivory had disappeared.

Barnabas had trailed her as far as Boston. But no one at the North Station or the South Station or Back Bay had seen a woman traveling with five white cats. He had gone to a radio station and they had broadcast a description of her. But Ivory Perry, age 33, height 5 feet 2, weight about 105 pounds, hair blond, eyes blue, had not been found.

This would be the first Christmas that Pam had not celebrated with Aunt Ivory. This would be the first year that a candlelit Christmas tree did not shine in Aunt Ivory's red plush parlor. It would not have been so bad, Pam thought, if only they knew where Aunt Ivory was. They had had just one postcard from her, a week ago. It was a picture of a row of palm trees with a moon shining on the water behind them. Underneath the picture were the words *Moonlight on the Water, Palmetto Beach, Fla.* On the other side Aunt Ivory had simply said, *Hope you all are fine. Love, Aunt Ivory.* That was all. She had never even said anything about Christmas.

They had come up to Twidboro the morning of Christmas Eve on the pretense of last-minute shopping. But, actually, deep in their hearts was the hope that somehow they would miraculously find Aunt Ivory home again. They had, in fact, come laden with gifts for her, just in case she was. But 11 Elm Street was locked and cold and empty. No wonder, then, that Pam had sounded wistful when Nancy talked of

Christmas in Twidboro.

"Better drink up your hot chocolate, kids. The stage leaves in five minutes," said Barnabas, smothering his red mustache in whipped cream. The three children buried their faces in their cups and in three minutes flat were out of the door with chocolate on their faces and burned tongues in their mouths.

"Merry Christmas, Nancy! Merry Christmas, Mr. Drake!" they shouted.

"Merry Christmas!" Nancy and her father called.

And the door banged behind Penny and Pam and Barney and Barnabas as they ran laden with Christmas packages to the corner where the stage was waiting to take them back to Abbidydumkeag. In spite of the disappointment of having to return to Indian Island with their presents for Aunt Ivory, the ride back in the stage was hilarious. Much of this was because of the jolly company of Mrs. Vinal who had also gone to Twidboro for last-minute purchases. All her children and her children's children were coming for Christmas dinner and on her lap sat a seventeen-pound turkey with only its legs in a pair of ruffled paper pantalettes protruding from the brown wrapping paper.

"Christmas presents?" she asked, as the girls plumped themselves beside her in the rear seat of the stage. Pam's and Penny's arms were filled with packages. "Can I ask what they are?"

"Yes," said Penny. "But I think we had better talk in code." Penny and Pam and Mrs. Vinal had a private language which they said was meant for ladies only. It was really very simple. All they did was to pronounce backward the words they did not want the others to hear.

"All right," said Mrs. Vinal. "What have you got for Appup?" (Appup, of course, was Puppa backward.)

"An ookcuc kcolc," said the twins together. They were going halves on the cuckoo clock because it was expensive.

"And some der skcos," said Pam.

"And a ralop raeb in a ebolg in a drazzilb," said Penny.

"I should think you three women would rather look out of the window and see the Christmas trees in front of the houses than torment us men with that fool language," called Barnabas from the front seat.

"We're doing both," laughed Mrs. Vinal. She turned back to Penny and Pam. "What have you got for Yenrab?"

"A tuocs efink," said Penny.

"And a citengam hsif dnop," said Pam, carefully feeling out the words "magnetic fish pond." They were hard to say backward.

"Wonderful!" cried Mrs. Vinal. "Now I'll tell you something. Can you keep a secret?"

"Oh, yes," said Penny and Pam in one breath.

"Well," said Mrs. Vinal slowly, "Yenrab's rehtaf and rehtom are going to be at my house for dinner tomorrow. They'll get here tomorrow morning. That's one reason I had to go up to Twidboro. For this," she said, patting with her red mitten the fat side of the turkey in her lap.

"Oh, Mrs. Vinal," breathed Pam. She had never seen Barney's mother and father. All she knew of them was from their letters and what Barney had told her of the two months he had spent with them in Florida the winter he was five years old. That was three years ago. And he had been too small to remember much. "Oh, Mrs. Vinal," she said again.

"Now, remember," said Mrs. Vinal, "not a word of this to Barney or your Puppa."

"What's all this?" Barnabas called. "Women are always having secrets. Who's coming to your house for dinner tomorrow?"

"Talk about the curiosity of women!" Mrs. Vinal laughed. "You'll see when you get there." For the Kellyhorns were having dinner at the boardinghouse tomorrow. "Let's sing," she said. "Pretty soon we won't be able to sing Christmas songs any longer."

WELCOME

Though Barney and Barnabas were burning with curiosity, they joined in the singing. The two men sitting on the middle seat of the stage turned out to be tenors from the choir of the church at Hatchet Cove. And Chick Gammage, the driver, fancied himself a baritone. So eight voices filled the old station wagon with "Deck the hall with boughs of holly, fol-la-la-la-la, la-la-la-la," as on Christmas Eve the stage rattled through the snowstorm down the river road to Abbidydumkeag. Nor did the singing stop when they reached Abbidydumkeag, but continued as Barnabas unerringly rowed them across the harbor through the swirling snowflakes and pulled the boat into the cleft in the rocks. And up the hill they went, singing "Jingle Bells." The snow fell all about them—on their heads and on their shoulders and on Barnabas's red eyebrows and mustache. It was snowing more heavily now. Only the juniper and blueberry bushes were yet uncovered.

"Some night for Santa Claus to be out in,"

shouted Barnabas, flinging open the kitchen door. They lit the kerosene lamps and prepared supper. No one paid much attention to eating, however. They were all too anxious to get at the tree. As soon as the dishes were done, Barnabas brought it in from the shed. They set it up in the parlor. It was a perfect tree—as tall as the room, and fat and bushy, and the needles were dark and shiny. It smelled delicious as it bathed in the warmth of the crackling fire on the hearth. Penny and Pam and Barney got the stepladder and loaded it to overflowing with garlands of white popcorn and red cranberries and colored paper chains. They hung the paper lanterns and then they put the candles on. Little white candles that Barnabas had bought at the Five and Ten. Barney had wanted to surprise his uncle by having the star already on, but in the end they couldn't reach the top of the tree despite the stepladder. So Barnabas had put it on himself. But he was none the less pleased.

When it was done they all went to get

their presents to put them under the tree for the morning. As they lowered themselves down the hatch, their arms overflowing with presents, they heard the sound of "Silent Night" coming from the old melodeon in the parlor. Barnabas was singing gently to himself as he played. His red hair shone in the firelight. And the room was filled with the magic of four dozen twinkling candles on a dark green Christmas tree.

CHAPTER TWELVE

The Merriest Christmas

IT HAD NOT yet grown light when Pam was rudely awakened by a series of thumps that caused her mattress to leap up and down. It was Penny punching the springs of her bed from the bunk below.

"Get up, sleepyhead," Penny called. "It's after six o'clock."

"Umpf," said Pam, turning over and burying her head beneath the quilt, as if thereby to escape the incessant pounding on her mattress. But Penny did not let up.

"It's past six o'clock," she repeated.

"'Stoo-early," Pam murmured, trying to sleep in the face of all these difficulties and nearly succeeding. But not quite. For the punches were raining faster than ever from the lower bunk.

"It's Christmas, dummy," Penny shouted.

And immediately Pam was wide awake. She sat up in bed and slammed her top of the window shut. Outside the window it was getting lighter. Penobscot Bay and the sky were so nearly the same shade of gray that it was impossible to tell where the sky left off and where the water began. Except for the hazy, darker gray outline of Vinalhaven in the distance, Pam could almost believe that all was sky and that she sat on the edge of the world. It had snowed a blizzard in the night and the snow lay deep on the ground. The spruce trees at the top of the island were so laden down with snow that the lower branches touched the ground, forming snowy tents beneath them. But the blizzard had stopped and only a light snow was falling now.

"Did someone say it was Christmas?" asked Barney, as he emerged sleepily around the end of the canvas wall that separated his room from theirs. His hair and blue pajamas were rumpled and his eyes were still full of sleep.

"I did," chanted Penny. "I did."

"And I do," echoed Pam, swinging her bare legs over the side of her bed.

"Oh, boy!" yelped Barney, making for the hatch. And they all stepped on each other's hands as they hastily lowered themselves down the rope ladder. They piled into the parlor. The tree was already lit, and there on the mantel-piece hanging before a roaring, crackling fire were their stockings. They were lumpy with presents, and a candy cane reared its head from the top of each of them.

"Wasn't that nice of Santa Claus to build a fire before he left!" cried Barney, falling upon his bulging stocking. "But I wonder how he got up the chimney again without burning his pants."

"My stocking looks as if it had the gout," exclaimed Penny, as she seized hers.

"Mine looks as if it had belonged to the fat lady at the circus," said Pam.

"I wish Mummy and Dad could be here for Christmas just once," said Barney wistfully at the mention of the circus.

"Maybe next year," said Pam, winking at Penny. What a Christmas this was going to be! Except that Aunt Ivory had vanished. Every silver cloud has a dark lining, Pam told herself, making up a new proverb.

"Look at Uncle Barnabas's stocking," said Barney sadly. "Santa Claus forgot all about him." Indeed, Barnabas's stocking hung as flat and as limp as when, at their insistence, he had hung it beside theirs the night before.

"How awful," whispered Pam. "We nearly forgot." She and Penny were up the rope ladder and through the hatch almost before she had finished speaking. In no time they were down again with the presents they had made for Barnabas's stocking—two little, sweet-smelling pillows, one stuffed with balsam needles, the other with sweet fern, a box of star-shaped cookies they had made in Mrs. Vinal's kitchen the Saturday before, a hemstitched handkerchief, a booklet of red and green blotters tied together with red ribbon and a sprig of bayberries that Pam had made at school, and a little calendar pasted on a piece of cardboard that was decorated around the edges with buttonhole stitches of red yarn.

"There," said Pam, stuffing Barnabas's stocking.

"My, Puppa has large feet," said Penny with dismay. For the stocking was only half full.

"I'll fix that," said Barney, running into the kitchen and coming back with four fat oranges. And, indeed, he did fix it. No stocking in the world had ever bulged more promisingly on Christmas morning.

"It's time to wake Puppa," said Penny. They went over to the door that opened into Barnabas's room.

"Let's sing 'Little Town of Bethlehem' this year," said Barney.

"All right," agreed Penny. So the three children stood outside Barnabas's door lustily singing Barney's favorite Christmas carol.

"Let's sing 'It Came Upon the Midnight Clear' just in case he didn't wake up," Pam suggested. The three of them were filled with the Christmas spirit. If the notes they sang were not all the correct ones, the carols were so joyful that the very mice in the walls must have danced for joy.

"I guess he's awake by now," said Barney, and they burst into Barnabas's room.

"Merry Christmas!" they shouted. Penny plopped Barnabas's bursting stocking on his chest.

"Merry Christmas to you," Barnabas replied. "What's this, anyhow?" he asked, reaching for his stocking. "I could swear that just before he went up the chimney I heard Santa Claus mutter, 'Barnabas Kellyhorn is too old for stockings.'"

Penny winked as she climbed into bed next to her father. "I think Mrs. Santa Claus kind of likes older men," she said.

"She must if she likes me," laughed Barnabas, holding the bedclothes open so that Pam and Barney could crawl in. And the four of them sat cozily in Barnabas's large four-poster bed as they emptied their stockings onto the patchwork quilt.

"Mrs. Santa Claus had quite a problem with my big feet," chuckled Barnabas, as the four oranges rolled into his lap. Penny and Pam and Barney squealed with excitement as the bulges in their stockings revealed themselves. There were chocolate creams as well as the candy canes, and a blue comb for Penny and a pink one for Pam, and Barney's stocking was filled with tricks—a pencil with a rubber point, tin cockroaches, rubber chewing gum, a fake ink spot, invisible ink, and a revolting, hairy, black spider.

"Wait till Miss Baker sees this!" he cried, as he unwrapped the spider.

There were many other presents too, and it

was nearly eight o'clock before they were through. The bed looked as though a hurricane had struck it.

"Boy! I'm hungry," said Barney, after he had rewrapped all his presents and stuck them back in his stocking. Later in the day, when the excitement was dying down, he intended to begin all over again on his stocking, pretending that it was only Christmas morning.

"Yes, let's get up and have breakfast," agreed Barnabas. "My stomach is talking. It's reminding me that Floyd sent over a hod of smelts for our Christmas breakfast."

Barnabas didn't have to say any more. For there is nothing more delicious than smelts fried in corn meal on Christmas morning. The four of them glutted themselves.

When breakfast was over, they took their fish-lined stomachs to the parlor and, sitting before the fireplace, unwrapped the packages from beneath the tree. There were fancy skates for Penny and Pam with white shoes and shining blades. And a pair of racing skates for Barney. Santa Claus had outdone himself this year, for, besides the skates, there were three pairs of skis. Only Barnabas knew that a Finn who lived in South Thomaston, had painstakingly planed and bowed and sandpapered six strips of ash wood, so that on Christmas morning, three pairs of polished skis could gleam in the parlor on Indian Island. There were other things besides these—long-needed mittens and underwear, and two charts from Barney, one for each twin. Pam's covered the Alewife River and Twidboro and Penny's showed the section of the Penobscot Bay in which Abbidydumkeag lay. Indian Island was marked with a little yellow star which meant that a lighthouse was there, for the chart had been printed before the light was discontinued.

There were other things besides. Writing paper from Nancy, books from Mrs. Vinal, and a catnip ball for Tiger Boy. The cuckoo clock Barnabas immediately hung in the place of honor above the table on which the family album rested.

"Cuckoo," called the wooden bird, popping its head out of a little wooden door in the clock. "Cuckoo," it called. Eleven times.

"Eleven o'clock already," cried Pam.

"We'd better go outside if we want to try our skis before lunch," Penny said.

"*Who* is it that's going to be at Mrs. Vinal's for lunch?" Barney asked inquisitively, while putting on his galoshes.

"Nobody special," said Penny with a chuckle.

The snow had stopped completely when they went outside. The sky had grown very light and there was a bright spot where the sun was trying to get through. The wind had come around from east to southwest so that perhaps by afternoon the sun would be shining. Indeed, the sun came out sooner than they had hoped. After an hour of breathlessly sliding down the hill, and stopping just before the cliffs only by falling in the deep, new powder snow, it was time to leave for Christmas dinner at Mrs.

Vinal's. As they rowed across the harbor, the wind shifted to somewhere between west and northwest. And a strip of pale blue sky opened up across the horizon behind Abbidydumkeag. It was cold out, and everyone's cheeks from exercise and the cold wind were the color of McIntosh apples as they stamped the snow off their feet and brushed each other off with the broom that Mrs. Vinal had conveniently placed beside the front door.

"There," said Barnabas, giving a final stamp with his big boots. He held open the door as the three children marched under his arm into Mrs. Vinal's front hall.

"Here they are now," Mrs. Vinal called over her shoulder to the guests in the front parlor. She rolled her plumply upholstered self down the hall to greet them. "Merry Christmas!" she cried. And she kissed them all. Even Barnabas. "I'm old enough to be his mother," she explained to the grinning children. "Here they are," she said again, ushering them into the parlor after they had hung their coats and mufflers on top of everyone else's on the clothes tree.

Crowded into the front parlor, along with an enormous, fat Christmas tree that was quite in keeping with the size of Mrs. Vinal, were Mrs. Vinal's children and all her children's children. Mrs. Vinal had five children herself and none of these had less than four children apiece and one even had nine. Besides these, Mrs. Vinal's children had each brought along their various husbands and wives.

"It's a good thing you keep a boardinghouse in the summer," Barnabas laughed. The room was large, but now it was packed with thirty people and a Christmas tree. Sixteen children had already overflowed into the back parlor.

"Do you know everybody?" asked Mrs. Vinal exclusively of Barney.

"I guess so," said Barney. He began politely to make his way around the room to shake everybody's hand. But he didn't get very far. He was only shaking the third hand when he found himself engulfed in the soft arms of a woman and the faint, familiar smell of lavender. He could have told from the perfume who it was though he looked up immediately.

"Mummy!" he cried. "Mummy, it's you!"

"Merry Christmas, darling," his mother replied. "I have a present for you, too."

"Two presents," quietly corrected the man standing behind her. He was a tall man. As tall as Barnabas. He had eyes like Barnabas's too. Bright blue and twinkling. And a smile of white teeth that stretched from ear to ear. That was as far as the resemblance went, but it was far enough for anyone to tell that the two men were brothers, even though one man's skin was tanned by the sun and his hair was blond, while the other man's skin was fair and his hair red.

"Dad!" cried Barney, falling on the tall man's neck. "Merry Christmas! Merry Christmas!"

"It certainly is a Merry Christmas," Conrad Kellyhorn replied, as he squeezed his son.

"Conrad!" cried Barnabas.

"Barnabas!" cried Conrad. "Merry Christmas."

The two brothers wrung each other's right hands while with the left hand they shook each other's shoulders.

"I hate to interrupt anything," interrupted Mrs. Vinal, "but I have four turkeys bursting with stuffing out in the kitchen, so . . ." She didn't have to say anything more, for her children's children were already on their feet and on their way to the dining room. Down the long room, where the boarders ate in the summer, stretched what seemed to be a mile of white-damask-covered table. Nothing was missing. At each end of the table gleamed a fat, golden brown turkey in white paper pantalettes. The table literally sagged with dishes of cranberry sauce and mountains of fluffy, mashed potatoes, with bowls of turnips and squash and every sort of vegetable that Mrs. Vinal had put up and stored in her larder for the winter. Boats of gravies and sauces, plates of hot biscuits, and dishes of nuts and candies added to the mouth-watering sight.

"I want the Kellyhorns all together at one end of the table, and we Vinals will sit at the other," shouted Mrs. Vinal above the hubbub. So Mrs. Vinal carved at her end of the table and Barnabas carved at theirs. When the carving was over they all fell to.

"That's some outfit you've got on, boy," Barnabas told Conrad, as he began his second helping of turkey. It was the second turkey, too.

"I'm a circus man," Conrad answered in his quiet voice. It was, indeed, "some outfit," and quite unlike the quiet Yankee who wore it. The coat was boldly checked in black and white, and beneath it he wore a pale yellow vest. "But this time next year," said Conrad, "things will be different."

Barnabas looked up from his plate. "How do you mean?" he asked.

"Lucy and I are leaving the circus after this next season."

"Is that the other Christmas present, Dad?" Barney asked, his eyes shining.

His mother and father both nodded their heads. Their eyes were shining too. Mrs. Conrad Kellyhorn was close to crying she was so happy.

"We've been foolish," Conrad Kellyhorn said regretfully. "Just because I ran away with the circus at thirteen, I always felt I was the black sheep and I didn't want to come home. When Barney came, well, there I was with a wife and child to support, and I knew of no other way to do it than by continuing to be a circus man. But we didn't want Barney to be a circus baby. It's no life for a child to be always on the move five months of the year—especially when the traveling often takes place at some ungodly hour of the night. That's why I asked you to board him. Besides, I wanted him to have the kind of childhood I had had on Indian Island when Puppa kept the light. I think of that time often. Some of the happiest moments of my life

I spent here in Abbidydumkeag. That's why Lucy and I are going to retire from the show business."

"But what can you do? How are you going to support your family?" asked Barnabas with a little pucker of worry between his eyebrows.

"I didn't want to say anything until everything was settled. But I saw old Ralph Middleby this morning and everything's fixed."

"You mean you're going to live here in Abbidydumkeag and help out at the general store?" asked Barnabas with a smile.

"Better still," said Conrad, also with a smile. "We're going to live in Abbidydumkeag and *own* the general store. Old Ralph says he's old enough to retire. And he says he'll be glad to give us advice until we amateur storekeepers have learned the business. How's that?"

"That," replied Barnabas, "makes this about the Merriest Christmas I have ever known."

At that point, dessert arrived. Desserts, rather. For there was squash pie and apple pie and mince pie and ice cream.

"Wonder you don't get stout," remarked Barnabas to Lucy Kellyhorn, as he watched her down her dessert.

"Exercise, I guess." Lucy Kellyhorn smiled up from the large wedge of apple pie before her. On top of it sat a generous mound of ice cream.

"All fooling aside, I should think it would be pretty hard work for a little thing like you. Especially learning new acts in the winter."

"Yes," she answered. "Yes, it is. But it's much more pleasant now that Conrad and I have taken a little house off in Plimpton. It's very quiet there."

"I had understood," Barnabas said, "that the circus winter quarters were in Plimpton."

Lucy Kellyhorn swallowed a piece of pie. "Oh, no," she said, "the winter quarters themselves are at Palmetto Beach."

Barnabas choked on his coffee. He choked and spluttered. And when he had finished, he carefully asked a question. "Did you ever meet anyone named Ivory Perry there?" he asked. "Kitty's sister. She has a lot of white cats."

Lucy Kellyhorn didn't answer at once. Her cheeks grew extraordinarily pink and she looked at Conrad. His face had a big "No" written across it. She looked down at her plate again and measured off a forkful of pie.

"No," she said. "No, I never did."

"That's funny," said Barnabas slowly. "I'm sure she's there. We had a postcard from her just the other day. I've been thinking that, after Christmas is over, I'd take a trip down there to bring her back."

"I wouldn't do that if I were you," said Conrad, looking up from his plate. "She isn't there. It's such a small town we would have met her if she were."

"Wel-ll," said Barnabas, "I don't know." But you could tell from his crestfallen face that he had been convinced.

CHAPTER THIRTEEN

Conrad's Story

IT WAS MIDAFTERNOON when, among a scraping of chairs and grunts of comfort and discomfort—depending upon how much the grunter had eaten—the Vinal clan and the Kellyhorn clan arose from the table. They made their way across the hall, praising the sumptuous feast as they went, and crowded themselves back into the parlor. The windows were filled with blue sky, and the bright sunlight, increased tenfold by the white snow, dimmed the splendor of the lightbulbs on the Christmas tree. The fifteen adults (for Nancy and Gramp—with a box of candy—had arrived at the end of the meal) took chairs, and the thirty-three children, by devious arrangements and rearrangements, each managed to find themselves a few square inches of sitting room on the floor of the parlor.

"Well," said Mrs. Vinal, when they were all settled, "who's going to tell us a story?" She brushed away some cake crumbs that were still sitting contentedly on her ample bosom.

"Yes," agreed Penny, "let's have a story."

"A true story," echoed Pam.

"That lets me out," chortled Gramp. "I know only fish stories."

"Count me out," said Nate Vinal, Mrs. Vinal's eldest son and father of five. "You've heard all my stories a hundred times."

"First time you ever admitted that," laughed his wife, who thought the number was closer to a thousand.

"What about Conrad here?" suggested Barnabas. "He must have a sleeve crammed full of stories that none of us have ever heard."

"Yes," they all chorused, turning to Conrad who sat on Mrs. Vinal's best, purple love seat beside the Christmas tree.

"We haven't seen you, Con, since that winter you were fifteen when you came home for a year," said Nate Vinal.

"But begin at the beginning, Dad, when you were thirteen," said Barney, who had heard the story before. "Begin where you saw the poster with the tigers on it."

"I've never been at such close quarters with an audience before," said Conrad, clearing his throat. "Lucy's and my act is high above everybody at the top of the tent. Even in the beginning when I started out I had room to move my big toe."

"Sorry, Dad," said Barney, who had been sitting on Conrad's big toe. He shifted as best he could.

"At the very beginning," Conrad began, "there was a circus poster pasted on a barn. The very same barn beside this house. It was a picture of black-striped tigers and yellow lions whose roaring mouths gaped like great, red caverns. In the cage with them was a golden-haired young hero dressed in white riding pants and armed only with a curling whip. It seemed as though one snap of the pointed, white teeth of any of the cats would have meant the end of the young man's life. Above the picture ran the words 'TOOTLE'S CIRCUS, The Only Show of its Kind on Earth.' That was a broad statement, but I believed it. Beneath the picture the poster said, 'Twidboro—July seventh—One Day Only.' Barnabas and I watched the man as he pasted the poster on the barn. We were nearly crazy with excitement for we had never seen a circus. And this was the closest any circus had ever come to Abbidydumkeag. The poster went up early in June and for a whole month Barnabas and I heckled everyone in town to give us odd jobs."

"I remember," nodded Mrs. Vinal, recalling how the two Kellyhorn boys kept knocking at her door to see whether she needed any kindling cut for the stove.

"I was so excited," Conrad continued, "that I kept borrowing Puppa's telescope. I used to sit on Indian Island with the telescope trained on Carrie Vinal's barn as I dreamed of July seventh. On July sixth we had saved up a dollar and a half between us. We started walking up the river road to Twidboro, for we hadn't enough money to treat ourselves to a ride up on the old stage. We spent the night with a great-aunt of ours in Twidboro and got up at the crack of dawn to see the circus tents go up. The stars were still faintly out as we made our way over to the hayfield where the circus was to be. Though already the cookhouse was up and a few black men were carrying pails of water to the animal wagons, the circus was still asleep. But not for long. As soon as the sun began to creep up over the horizon to dry the dew on the hayfield, the circus wagons came to life, and the bustle and commotion of getting up the big top started. A circle of stakes was driven into the ground by four black men. One after the other they would hit each stake as they sang to the rhythm of their heavy mallets. And then they would go on to the next stake. Barnabas and I wanted to do something too, so we went up to a man in a straw hat who seemed to be directing the operations. He was a thin man with a wry face and he wore a vest and a pair of lavender elastic bands to hold up his shirtsleeves.

"'Job, boys?' he asked, even before we spoke. 'Go over to that wagon near the elephants and tell that little man Mr. Tootle said to give you a job.' He never looked at us once while he spoke. Our mouths dropped open. This was the great Mr. Tootle! Though he seemed not to take his eyes from the circle of stakes into which the canvas of the big top was to be hauled, he must have seen our look of incredulity, for something like a smile was twitching on his mouth. 'Get along with you,' he said gruffly. 'Can't have any loafers hanging around. Now git.' And we got. 'Don't forget to come back and see me when you're through,' he called after us.

"Barnabas and I went over to the little man.

"'Sir, Mr. Tootle said—' I began.

"'All right,' he interrupted. 'Let's see,' he said, scratching the three days' growth of beard on his chin. 'How about carrying water for the elephants?'

"'That would be fine,' we said. And we started.

"'This is pie,' Barnabas said. I agreed. But by ten-thirty our opinion had changed. Four and a half hours of carrying big buckets of water for elephants was hard work. In one sniff, an elephant would suck up a pailful. Half the time he had the irritating habit of squirting it in the air and using it for a shower bath instead of drinking water. However, ten-thirty did come, and the performers were all in their wagons getting ready for the eleven o'clock parade. Barnabas and I found Mr. Tootle in his private wagon leaning back in a swivel chair with his feet propped up on a desk containing two black ledgers and a tall pile of pink handbills to distribute among the crowd at the parade. There was a calendar on the wall above the desk and a fat black stove in one corner. It looked very much the same as any other office except that behind the door was a cot with a sagging mattress and Mr. Tootle's nightshirt hanging on a nail.

"'Come in, boys,' Mr. Tootle said, without looking up from the contemplation of the long ash on his black cigar. 'I'll be right with you,' he said, waving us to a seat on the cot. We sat there for five long minutes while Mr. Tootle watched the progress of his cigar ash. Suddenly he swung abruptly around in his swivel chair. 'That's where they all sit,' he said sadly. 'That's where they all sit when they want to get paid. You don't think I could make that hole in the mattress all by myself, do you?'

"'No, sir,' we said.

"'And when the Fat Lady comes for her wages, she doesn't help matters much,' he went on morosely. 'I suppose that's what you're here for?'

"'No, sir,' we said. 'We just wanted to

help. And you said to come see you when we were through.'

"'So I did,' he said. 'So I did.'

"Nobody said anything while Mr. Tootle pushed his straw hat to the back of his head.

"'So we just came,' Barnabas finished lamely.

"The same wry smile flickered over Mr. Tootle's face. 'Boys after my own heart,' he said. He pulled two yellow pieces of cardboard out of his vest pocket. Written on them was the word PASS in black, important letters. Mr. Tootle handed us each one. 'Hope you enjoy the show,' he said, dismissing us as he swung around to the desk.

"'Oh, we will, sir,' we answered, leaving the great Mr. Tootle flicking his two-inch ash into an ashtray. We headed for Main Street through which the parade was to pass. And pass it did in all its splendor. First came the horses, the thick-bodied, plump, white horses of the bareback riders. But now they were decked in cloth of gold, and pom-poms nodded on their heads. Each one bore on his back a beautiful girl in a short, silver-spangled dress, perched precariously with delicately crossed legs and pointed toes. Some of the Twidboro ladies thought their clothes indecent, but they were a pretty sight. Behind the white horses came the clowns with their painted faces. They ran back and forth out of line blowing up balloons until they burst, tripping over each other, and handing out the pink handbills to the crowd. Behind the clowns were three little, red goat carts with yellow wheels that carried midgets who, though it was broad daylight, were elaborately bedecked in evening clothes and jewelry. After them walked the other freaks—the Fat Lady and her husband the Blue Man; the Living Skeleton; Blubbo the Voracious Cannibal from the Dark Heart of Africa; and Pierre the Alligator Boy. On the heels of the freaks came the strident music of the steaming calliope. Four spirited, black stallions with red plumes on their heads drew the shining brass boiler. The cages containing the wild animals came next. And there were my wild lions and tigers! They were paying no attention to the music or the crowd but remained curled up and dreaming behind the bars. Our elephants came next. On their backs beneath fringed canopies were the very black men who had driven the stakes for the big top. But now the men wore purple and red capes and golden crowns set with pearls. And at the end of the parade came the cowboys in fur chaps chasing wildly in and out of each other on their small, brown-and-white horses.

"The reason I tell you all this," Conrad Kellyhorn explained, "is that all these people were to take the place of my father and mother and brother in the years that followed.

"Well," he went on, "Barnabas and I went to the circus with our passes in the afternoon and we had money enough to go again that night. I was even more taken with the circus the second time than the first. The upshot of the matter was that after the show was over, I hunted up Mr. Tootle and told him I wanted to join up with them. He not only agreed to take me on, but he had another cot moved into his own wagon that very night. And the next morning I woke up in the office of the great Mr. Tootle as it went along to its next one-night stand. I guess it was tough on Barnabas who had to break the news to Mumma and Puppa."

Barnabas nodded his head.

"The first two years," Conrad continued, "I was just a chore boy. I loved it but I grew homesick. So when I was fifteen I came back to Indian Island for a year. But the circus, even though it was not as glamorous behind the scenes, had got into my blood. I wanted to go back. However, the idea of spending the rest of my life carrying water for the ungrateful elephants didn't appeal to me. So I would climb through the hatch to my room and, pulling the rope ladder up after me so that I couldn't be followed, I would practice. Mr. Tootle had once mentioned that he was looking around for a sword swallower. So I decided that that was what I would be. Up in my room on Indian Island I learned my trade."

"Didn't it make you feel sick the first time, Uncle Conrad?" asked Penny practically, thinking of how she hated it when Dr. Cox was fooling around her throat with a tongue depressor.

"Not only the first time. It was six months before I could do it without being sick."

"Ugh," said one of Mrs. Vinal's children's children, feeling a little ill, what with the big Christmas dinner and all.

"Anyhow, I went back to the circus that spring in the position of sword swallower. And Mr. Tootle donated a pair of green tights to the cause. I don't believe any of you ever knew this. Mumma was always a little ashamed of it. She never would come to see me though once Puppa did. I think he kind of liked my act," said Conrad with a blush. "At any rate, I was only at it a few years. Lucy, whose father was head of the Wild West Show, was a great friend of mine. On the side we were perfecting a perch act together. At the end of three years it was good enough for Mr. Tootle. We celebrated by getting married." Conrad smiled across the room at his wife. "It wasn't till after Barney arrived that we started working out our flying act. That's different from a perch act, in that for a flying act you use two trapezes instead of one and you change from one to the other in midair. We've worked it up so that now we never use a net. Funny about the public," he said. "No matter how tricky you are, if you use a net, they don't gasp at all. I guess they imagine that there's no danger and it's fun to fall into a net. It may look soft and bouncy from where they sit. But it really hits you pretty hard, and if you don't know how to fall just right, you're liable to break your back. We don't even have the net now, because our timing is perfect. If it weren't, we wouldn't be here for Christmas today," Conrad Kellyhorn concluded.

The last rays of the afternoon sun were shining over the top of the hills behind Abbidydumkeag. The hills themselves were blue with their own shadows and the trees and buildings in the sun cast long shadows toward the harbor.

"Barney's Christmas present!" Lucy Kellyhorn exclaimed. "We nearly forgot. And the stage will soon be here." She stood up and left the room.

"That was a wonderful story," Mrs. Vinal's children's children were saying, as Lucy Kellyhorn came back from the shed. "Will you swallow a sword for us?"

"Next year when I'm carving my own Christmas turkey at my own house in Abbidydumkeag I'll swallow the carving knife. After I'm done carving, of course. All who care to witness the spectacle are cordially invited," answered Conrad. "But here is Barney's present."

At that moment Mrs. Kellyhorn entered the room. Following daintily behind her was a small, cloven-hoofed animal with knobby knees. From a red ribbon around its neck hung a little tag. Suddenly the little white animal leaped high in the air and, jumping over all the legs on the floor, went right to Barney.

"What is it?" Barney asked, his eyes shining. "Is it all mine?"

"Every last hair," said his father, as the little animal tried to nibble at Barney's ear. "Read the tag."

"Don't move so much, boy. I want to read your tag." And Barney read:

"My father pulled a red cart
The wheels of which were yellow.
I'm much too small for any dwarf,
So you're the lucky fellow.

"Oh, Dad," he said, "it's one of the midgets' goat's babies! " It was a mouthful.

"Merry Christmas," answered his father, just before he went down for the third time under Barney's wet kisses. The room was almost dark now. The only light came from the sunset, the fire in the fireplace, and the colored lights on Mrs. Vinal's tree. Everyone was quietly and happily talking with one another. Then above the voices the clanking of an automobile's chains was heard.

"I'm afraid that's the stage, Lucy," Conrad Kellyhorn said.

Beep, beep, sounded a horn in front of Mrs. Vinal's boardinghouse. Though Lucy and Conrad did not know it, the stage did not usually run on Sundays or holidays. And never before on Christmas. It was Chick Gammage's Christmas present to the Kellyhorns.

"I guess you're right, dear," said Lucy Kellyhorn.

The Kellyhorns, with the Vinals trailing behind them, followed Conrad and Lucy into the hall. Everyone tried to help them as they struggled into their coats and mufflers.

"I guess I'll have to buy me some galoshes

next year," Lucy Kellyhorn laughed, looking down at her pretty feet in their thin slippers.

"Dad," asked Barney, "can I call my goat after Mr. Tootle?"

"I rather think he'd like it," replied his father, kissing him good-bye.

Beep, beep, sounded the horn as once again Lucy Kellyhorn enveloped her son in the faint smell of lavender.

"Good-bye! Good-bye!" everyone called, as Mr. and Mrs. Conrad Kellyhorn ran down the path to the stage. Across the harbor the windows of the house and the lighthouse on Indian Island still shone pink in the sunset.

"It certainly has been a Merry Christmas," said Barnabas.

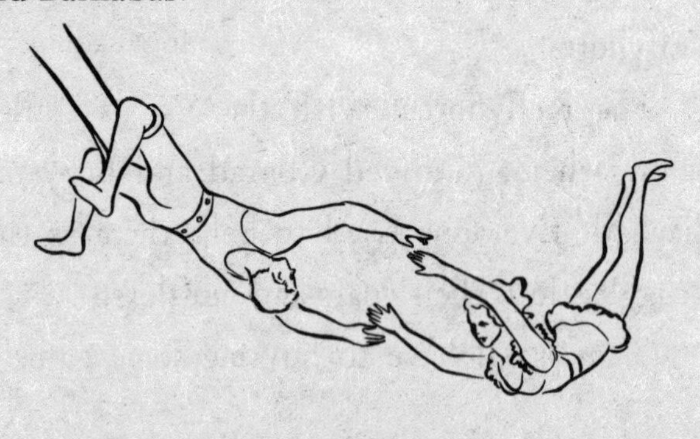

CHAPTER FOURTEEN

The Accident

TO PENNY AND Pam and Barney it seemed that their Christmas vacation was over almost before it began. It was the last day of vacation now, and tomorrow at this time they would be sitting at their desks in school, their tin lunch boxes open before them as they undid the old bread wrappers that held their sandwiches. Lunch was always the best part of school. It was like having a picnic every day. But it was a poor picnic compared to the one they were having today at Spectacle Pond. Spectacle Pond was really two ponds joined together by a little strip of water so that on a map it looked like a pair of spectacles. It lay halfway up the river road to Twidboro, a question of ten miles, and the Kellyhorns had got a ride up with Nate Vinal and his five children who were staying at their grandmother's for the Christmas vacation. Gramp had come down in the truck with Nancy in front and five brooms and four snow shovels and six of Pam's former classmates bundled to the ears in back.

They had spent the morning clearing the left-hand lens of the spectacles. Underneath the snow was what Nate called "black ice"—ice frozen on so still a night that the surface was like glass and the ice so clear they could see right through it to the dark depths of the pond. When they were through it was lunchtime. Gramp had started a bonfire on the bank at the narrow end of the pond where the left lens joined the right. A steaming pot of cocoa was balanced on a rock, and there were hot dogs and marshmallows for them to roast. Not much variety. But quantity made up for it.

"Come 'n' get it," shouted Gramp to the weary red-cheeked shovelers and sweepers.

And come they did. And got it.

"I wish we'd brought Mr. Tootle," said Barney, stuffing a roll full of mustard and hot dog into his mouth. They had left Mr. Tootle with Mrs. Vinal because, like a baby, he had to have his bottle every three hours.

"I don't think Mr. Tootle would be very good at hockey," said Pam. They had all brought their skates and hockey sticks. The twins had brought their new, white skates and Barney his racing ones. They hadn't used them yet because there had been so much snow on all the ponds. Besides, they had been busy sliding on their new skis. But after lunch they put them on.

"Here goes Sonja Henie!" cried Penny, running out onto the ice on the tips of her fancy skates. "Watch!" she called, as she glided on the blades. And down she went. Flat on her face.

"Better take a lesson from me!" advised Pam, following Penny out onto the ice. And down she went flat on her face. The two girls sat up and looked at each other. Pam's face was puzzled. She had skated ever since she could remember.

"It's the teeth," Penny explained. "They catch if you lean too far forward."

"I guess we'll have to learn to skate all over again," said Pam. "We can't let Barney be a better skater than us." They looked up at Barney who was skating circles around them and grinning from ear to ear. Around and around he went, cutting his edges, his arms complacently folded behind his back. The fact that he skated on his ankles mattered not a whit to him. The Vinals and the children from Twidboro were already out on the ice with their hockey sticks and a puck, warming up for the big game. But Gramp was still busy with the fire. So Penny and Pam stumbled over to an unused corner to find out what it was that they did wrong.

"Even if it takes me all night," said Pam, after an especially hard crack of skull on ice, "I'm going to find out how to work these things."

"You didn't call them 'things' on Christmas

morning," said Penny, recalling Pam's glee when she unwrapped the shining white skates.

But it didn't take them all night. Within an hour they had conquered the art of not leaning too far forward. Gramp swooped toward them on his old-fashioned rockers, making grapevines on the ice as he came. He swished to a stop an inch away in a shower of ice particles.

"You're both captains," he said. "We're about to start."

The game was soon under way. A good game it was, too, save for some grave moments when the teams couldn't tell the two captains apart. Shouts of triumph and dismay mingled with the cutting of the blades and the sudden scraping as the skaters changed direction with the puck. These sounds rose to join the afternoon cawing of the crows who watched the game from the tops of the spruce trees. The sun sank early behind the trees, but the hockey players played on. When they did stop it was only because they could no longer see the puck.

It was still darker, almost night, when the three Kellyhorns waited on the wharf in Abbidydumkeag while Floyd untied the painter of his dory.

"Your Puppa started off late to haul his traps. He asked me to row you out if he wasn't back when you came," Floyd had informed them, between chews on his quid. The Kellyhorns stood patiently with their new skates hanging on the hockey sticks over their shoulders. Against Barney's chest Mr. Tootle contentedly rubbed the place where his horns would be coming through, his legs dangling from his master's arms.

"Puppa will be along soon," said Pam. "We can have a good supper waiting for him." Pam's stomach was growling again.

"Maybe he'll be home when we get there," said Penny hopefully, though no light came from the windows of the house on the island. And when Floyd brought the dory into the cleft in the rocks it was empty save for the white ice on the cliffs and the ring in the rock to which Barnabas tied his dory.

"Let's hurry and be ready for him when he comes," Pam cried, racing up the hill to the house. The two girls put on slippers and tied their aprons over their ski pants before they went about the business of preparing supper. Barney was sitting in the middle of the kitchen floor giving Mr. Tootle his bottle. He still wore his heavy sweater and his toboggan cap.

"I think I'll have one last slide down the hill before vacation is over," he explained.

"But it's night out!" exclaimed Pam.

"Maybe you ought to ask Puppa when he comes," suggested Penny.

Mr. Tootle sucked hopefully on the nipple of the empty bottle.

"It's bedtime, you greedy goat," said Barney rising and teasing the goat into the shed by wagging the bottle before its nose. "There," he said, coming back with his skis. "Please, can't I go? We've got the hill packed down just perfect. And it might snow tonight. I know my way down the hill with my eyes closed."

"Well," said Penny, as she relented even though there wasn't a chance of snow with the wind the way it was.

"Well," said Pam, giving in. She wouldn't have minded a slide down the hill herself. But there was supper to get. "Just once," she said. "And be careful."

Barney let in a cold puff of air as he slammed the door behind him. Penny and Pam thought no more about the matter. There was work to be done in the kitchen. Potatoes to peel. Carrots to pare. And the last of a leg of lamb to cut up. There was going to be stew for supper tonight.

"The tag end of vacation and the tag end of the lamb," Pam sang tunelessly, as she hacked away at the meat.

Penny decided to make some johnnycake since Barnabas had not yet come home. They put the stew on the stove and the johnnycake in the oven. And still Barnabas was not home. Tiger

Boy thought he had been forgotten and emerged from behind the stove mewing for his supper.

"I wonder where Puppa can be," said Pam, giving Tiger Boy some milk. "He ought to have been home long ago even if he did start late."

"Do you think we should start eating when supper's ready?" asked the famished Penny.

"We ought to wait for Barney, anyhow," said Pam.

"That's right," said Penny. "He ought to be back by now."

"I guess he decided he'd go down the hill more than once," said Pam. "I'll go call him." She put on her galoshes without fastening them and stuck her arms into her heavy coat.

"I'll watch the johnnycake," Penny told Pam, as she went out into the night. There was no moon, but the black sky was alive with stars. It was very dark out despite the white snow. Pam made her way slowly up the hill. The snow was deceiving. Without shadows to outline the bumps and hollows it seemed only a sea of white. Pam's eyes could see no dips or rises but her feet found them all. Twice she fell down.

"Barney," she called, when she neared the top of the hill.

But there was no answer. Barney must be at the bottom of the hill. Pam started down. Her galoshes kept trying to slide from beneath her, for the snow was packed down hard. She dug her heels in, thinking how displeased Barney would be in the morning when he saw the smooth hill marred with footprints. Anyhow, she thought, they couldn't be as bad as the deep holes Barney made when he fell hurtling into the snow.

"Barney!" she called again. Again no one answered. Pam went all the way to the bottom of the hill calling his name. But Barney never answered. Pam felt suddenly frightened standing alone at the edge of the sea of whiteness with only the rote of the ocean at the bottom of the cliffs to keep her company.

"Barney!" she called again. But not so loudly as before. She thought to herself that it sounded more like the frightened bleat of Mr. Tootle than her own voice. Still there was no answer.

He probably went right back to the house from here, she told herself. I must have missed him when I went to the top of the hill. She was just about to turn back to the house herself when she heard a small noise from the direction of the cliffs.

"Barney!" she called experimentally. The noise sounded again. It was a small, plaintive whimper from below the cliffs. Pam went to the edge of the rocks. Her heart was thudding heavily under her coat and her breath came fast. "Barney," she called, "where are you?"

"Here," said a small voice from the top of another cliff which lay some fifteen feet below the first one. Pam could see a little figure sitting huddled up in the snow. Somehow she managed to climb down to him.

"It's my foot," Barney said in a little voice. "I

can't stand on it. I thought you'd never come." His skis, or what had been his skis, lay beside him. The tip of one was broken off and the other was split clean in two.

If only Puppa were here, Pam thought in despair. "What happened?" she asked Barney.

"I only went down once like you said. The snow looked so funny I couldn't tell exactly where I was. Suddenly there were the cliffs. I tried to stop like you showed me. And then I was here. And something happened to my foot."

Pam's arms were around him now. He started to cry. "And I broke both my skis," he sobbed.

"Maybe Puppa can get you another pair," said Pam. "Here. Put your arm around my shoulders and we'll try to get back to the house."

Pam lifted and boosted Barney up the steep rock, staying behind to catch him should he slip. Slowly and painfully they made their way back to the house. Penny was dishing out three bowls of stew when Barney hobbled in.

"Barney!" she cried when she saw his white face.

"It's just my foot," said Barney manfully. But the two girls put him to bed, in Barnabas's room because it would have been impossible to get him up the rope ladder to his own bed.

"How do you feel now?" asked Pam, tucking him in.

"Fine," said Barney. But the twins knew it was a lie, because his foot had already swollen to twice its normal size. "Just like my stocking on Christmas morning," Barney had said, trying to make a joke.

"If only Puppa were here," Penny said. They had ceased worrying about him now that Barney was hurt. They were sitting now on his bed eating stew and johnnycake with Barney. But their appetites had disappeared. Barney hardly touched his food. When they were through they turned the lamp low so that he could sleep and went back to the kitchen.

"What should we do?" asked Pam. "The

dory's gone so we can't go in town for Dr. Cox."

"If only we could signal them some way. But they can't see us waving anything at night."

"Except a lantern," said Pam. "I learned the Morse code at the Girl Scouts in Twidboro."

"You can do it from the lighthouse. They'd notice that," said Penny hopefully.

By this time Barney was delirious. He called to them and when they came he said worriedly, "There's a goat skiing on my bed. Brush him off, please, Pam."

"There," said Pam, pretending to brush away the imaginary goat. "And if he does come back, it's only Mr. Tootle." She said it gently and comfortingly. But leaving Penny holding Barney's hand, she hurried into her coat and, taking a lantern, went up the winding stairs to the top of the cold lighthouse.

"S O S," she signaled. And then she spelled out "D-o-c-t-o-r C-o-x." For an hour she stood in the top of the tower raising and lowering the lantern. Dot, dot, dot; dash, dash, dash; dot, dot, dot. Over and over she signaled it. "S O S. D-o-c-t-o-r C-o-x. S O S." She stood alone, praying under her breath that someone would see it or that Barnabas would come home. She could hear only her own breathing and the waves crashing beyond the lighthouse. And then, joining these, she thought she heard another sound. As it came nearer she could make out the *clop clop* of someone in a rowboat.

"Thank you! Thank you!" she called to God. She ran down the spiral staircase and across the snow to the cleft in the rocks to catch the painter of the dory.

CHAPTER FIFTEEN

The End of the Boardinghouse

"PENNY-PAM," CAME Barnabas's voice in the dark. "Is that you?"

"It's me," said Pam, reaching for the painter.

"What happened?" Barnabas asked. "I brought Dr. Cox with me."

"It's Barney," Pam told them, as Barnabas hauled the dory up over the ice-caked rocks. "He hurt his leg." She told them about it as they went up to the house.

"Hmm," said Dr. Cox. He wasn't given a great deal to the practice of talking.

"We thought you'd never come," Pam told Barnabas, her mittened hand in his big leather glove.

"I stayed to supper up to Lem Trott's."

Lemuel Trott had a trucking business at Hatchet Cove. Every other night, when the highway was least crowded, he drove a big red truck, filled with eggs from the hen farms of the county, a hundred and eighty-five miles to the market in Boston. "But I'll tell you about that later," Barnabas said, for they had reached the kitchen door. Barnabas hung his checked windbreaker and corduroy cap on a nail behind the door and set a big pasteboard box on the kitchen table. Penny helped Dr. Cox off with his sheepskin coat and took his beaver hat. Then with his little black bag he and Barnabas followed her into the bedroom. Barney looked very little in the big bed. His cheeks were flushed and his eyes were very bright.

"He looks a lot better," said Penny, remembering how white his face had been when he had limped in.

"A little too well," grunted Dr. Cox, for Barney's rosy cheeks and too bright eyes were feverish. "Let's see the leg," he said gently, turning back the bedclothes. The leg, if possible, was still more swollen, and the ankle was as large as the calf. "Try to move your toes," said the doctor. But Barney couldn't. "Looks broken," said Dr. Cox tersely to Barnabas, as Penny and Pam tiptoed out of the room.

Barney had fainted clear away when Dr. Cox set the bone, Barnabas told them, after he came back from rowing the doctor home. Barney was asleep now in the big bed, his leg stuck stiffly out in splints and bandages.

"It's my fault," said Penny. "I shouldn't have let him go."

"It's just as much mine as yours," said Pam miserably. It was a dismal end to a glorious vacation. The fun they had had these two weeks had nearly erased the hurt Pam had felt because Aunt Ivory had forgotten her on Christmas. But it all came back to her now. Her eyes filled with tears, but she refused to cry.

"There, now," said Barnabas, taking her on his knee. "Accidents like that are no one's fault.

Almost every boy breaks an arm or a leg sometime or other.

"If it will make you feel any better," he added, "there's a box for a Miss Pamela Kellyhorn on the table. Lem Trott brought it down from the express office in Twidboro on his way back from Boston. It's been sitting there since Christmas Eve. For all they care it could sit there till Easter."

Pam slid off his knee and ran to the kitchen table. The tag on the box read: *From I. Perry, Twidboro, Maine. To Miss Pamela Kellyhorn, Indian Island, Abbidydumkeag, Maine.* But the label showed that it had been sent from Florida.

"Oh," she said. "Oh." And she burst into tears. She had refused to cry when she was worried and frightened, and now, in her relief, for the first time in her life she cried for joy. Because Aunt Ivory had not forgotten her. Nor had she forgotten Penny and Barney and Barnabas; there were presents for them as well as for her. There was a coconut for each of them and thin little vials of orange blossom perfume for the girls. A snakeskin belt for Barnabas and netting bags filled with nuts. Another box contained shells from the shore, shells just as pretty as the ones from the South Sea Islands that sat on the parlor mantelpiece. Last of all, there was a mysterious box for Barney with something inside that jingled when you shook it.

"I wonder what it is," Penny said. It was late, but they were still lying awake and talking. Pam could never do this at the Drakes' because there the walls were paper-thin. In this case, however, there was a sturdy floor between them and Barnabas so their drowsy murmuring went unheeded. Pam lay in the bunk above, wondering too. But her thoughts were of a somewhat different nature.

"You know," she said, "it's queer about Aunt Ivory."

"You mean because she never writes?"

"Well, yes, that. But I was thinking about her sending us that postcard from the same town where Uncle Conrad's circus is."

"She couldn't be living there," said Penny, "or she'd have answered the letter you wrote to Palmetto Beach by now. Besides, I heard Puppa ask Aunt Lucy if she'd ever met her. And she said no."

"I heard her too," said Pam. "But she sort of hemmed and hawed before she answered."

"You're just imagining things," Penny yawned. "It must be awful late. I think I'll go to sleep. Good night."

"Good night," said Pam, who was still wide awake. "You know," she said a minute later, "Barney won't have to go to school with his broken leg."

"Mmmmm-rrrrr," said Penny.

Every cloud had a silver lining, Pam told herself, going back to the old tried and true before she burrowed under her pillow and went to sleep.

Nor was that the only happy purpose that Barney's fractured ankle served.

The following day Barnabas rowed Barney across the harbor to Abbidydumkeag where Dr. Cox put Barney's leg and foot into a hard white cast of plaster of Paris. Mrs. Vinal donated a small pair of crutches from her attic that Nate had used years ago after he had broken his leg jumping in the hay loft. Barney's leg pained him the first few days and his armpits ached because he was new at using crutches. He still slept in Barnabas's bed for, although he managed to hop all over the ground floor, there was no way of getting him up through the hatch to his own bedroom. Barnabas was too big for Barney's little bunk, so the two of them shared the bedroom on the ground floor. It was at night that Barney's leg troubled him most. The cast which Dr. Cox had put on, besides being hard and white, was a large, cumbersome affair and very heavy as well. Every time he attempted to turn over, the weight of his leg pinned him down in such an uncomfortable position that he woke up. When morning came he felt as though he hadn't slept all night.

One night, about a week after the accident, when everyone in the house on Indian Island was dead to the world, Barney, curled up next to his softly snoring uncle, attempted in his sleep to uncurl with the usual result. Now, Barnabas's room was on the west side of the house facing the harbor, with the bed right under the window, so when Barney, who was sleeping with his face to the wall, woke up he was looking across the harbor to the sleeping village of Abbidydumkeag. For a minute Barney was not sure whether he was awake or asleep. He thought he saw a row of Christmas candles running along the ridge pole of Mrs. Vinal's roof. He rubbed his eyes. The Christmas candles were still there. But they weren't candles. They were little tongues of flame dancing along the roof top.

"Uncle Barnabas!" he cried, pulling at the sleeve of Barnabas's nightshirt.

"Mmmm-rrr," said Barnabas.

"Uncle Barnabas, Mrs. Vinal's house is on fire!"

"FIRE!" shouted Barnabas, sitting up in bed. "Good grief! So it is." He was out of bed and pulling his pants up over his nightshirt without more ado.

Pam and Penny had heard him cry out. They came tumbling down the ladder with their clothes under their arms for they thought their own house was on fire.

"It's Mrs. Vinal's boardinghouse," said Barney excitedly. Penny and Pam put their ski pants on over their pajamas. They were going along whether Barnabas knew it or not.

"Will you be all right, Barney?" they asked.

"Sure," said Barney politely, though his eyes were filled with envy.

The wind was blowing hard from the north as the dory crossed the harbor. And all the stars were shining. Indeed, there was not a trace of a cloud for them to hide behind.

"It's the chimney," said Barnabas. A torrent of sparks was pouring from Mrs. Vinal's chimney and falling like golden rain on the roof. The whole roof was on fire when they reached the wharf. Heavy, ominous smoke coiled from beneath the shingles. Here and there a sly tongue of flame darted forth licking the edge of one of them.

"FIRE!" shouted Barnabas, stopping to pound on Floyd's door as they ran up the hill.

"FIRE! FIRE!" they shouted, running along the road. Heads appeared at the windows. From the doors rushed men, pulling up their pants as they went, and women with only coats over their nightdresses. One or two senseless children ran out, forgetting even their bedroom slippers. The telephone operator was wakened from her midnight snooze by five frantic telephone calls for the engine at Hatchet Cove, the nearest town that boasted a fire department. Before Barnabas and the girls could reach the boardinghouse, the heavy smoke had fulfilled its promise. The little tongues of flame, aggravated by the wind blowing hard out of the north, suddenly burst forth with a roar of defiance. A hundred feet away they could feel the scorching heat from the hungry fire. Next to its lurid light the moon was only a feeble little fingernail in the sky.

"Stay out here and keep out of the way," Barnabas directed Pam and Penny, as he went into the burning house. Smoke was already gushing from Mrs. Vinal's half-open bedroom window. The twins stood close together, holding each other by the hand. There were other men going into the house now, some with hatchets and others with pails of water. Still others went in and came out again, carrying pieces of furniture which they placed in the road swarming with fascinated onlookers. Floyd came out with Mrs. Vinal's best, purple love seat.

"Here, you two," he said to Penny and Pam, "you might as well be comfortable."

"Thank you," they said, with their eyes still on the men who kept coming out of the burning building. Finally they saw Barnabas. At first they thought it was a mattress which he had slung over his shoulder. On closer examination, it proved to be Mrs. Vinal, who had been overcome with smoke as she lay asleep. Barnabas had wrapped her in a pink blanket.

"Let me down, you young ruffian," said the struggling Mrs. Vinal, as Barnabas carried her toward them. "I have two good feet of my own to walk on."

"You're not in any condition—" began Barnabas in a fatherlike voice, though he was young enough to have been her son. But at that point Mrs. Vinal wriggled loose and dropped with a thud to the ground.

"Lord, have pity on us!" she exclaimed, turning to look at her flaming house. "My new sewing machine!" Before Barnabas could stop her, Mrs. Vinal in a nightcap, with the pink blanket streaming behind her, was flying back into the burning house. The windows on the second floor had now all been smashed by hatchets.

"I'll bet they never thought of opening them," said Barnabas.

Wicked yellow flames shot forth, devouring what remained of the windows. Volumes of black smoke poured continuously into the sky, completing the obliteration of the moon. To Penny and Pam on the purple love seat, Abbidydumkeag seemed like a stage set which consisted only of the fronts of houses brilliantly lit by orange footlights.

"Dear me," said Mrs. Vinal, setting her sewing machine on the ground and sitting down beside them. "I hope the Hatchet Cove engine gets here soon. The house is half gone now." As she spoke, the ridgepole gave way. A vivid mountain of fire rose to the sky as the flaming roof tore itself loose from its timbers and sank into what had once been Mrs. Vinal's attic. The men worked more furiously than ever. There were three lines for passing buckets of water into the house, but they made little headway against the blaze. Abbidydumkeag boasted not one hook ladder, not a foot of hose, nor a single force pump. They were totally unprepared for a fire of this magnitude. Finally they heard the siren of the engine from Hatchet Cove come screaming down the river road. The tires of the hurtling engine screeched to a stop.

"Ma," called the fire chief, climbing down from the engine. "Ma, where are you?" It was Nate Vinal. One of the crowd pointed to the purple love seat. Nate, with relief, turned back to his men. "She's got a well behind the house," he told them.

"It's almost dry," called a man from one of the bucket-passing lines.

Nate's face fell. Mrs. Vinal's boardinghouse stood by itself apart from the other houses. The hose could not possibly reach to her closest neighbor's. "The nearest water," he said, "is down in the harbor."

"It's no use," said one of his men. "The hose won't reach."

"Besides," said another, "it's all going to go soon. A house like this is like kindling wood. It'll be gone by the time we get the water."

"At least we can save the barn," said Nate desperately. A valiant little bucket brigade, headed by Barnabas, was trying to keep the barn wet so that it would not catch fire in the intense heat. The first fireman who had answered Nate was wrong. The hose did reach the harbor. But the second man was right. It had taken a long time to reach the water. The bank below the boardinghouse was very steep and still deep with snow. It was just as the first salt water came gushing through the nozzle that Mrs. Vinal's boardinghouse sank to the ground and its flaming timbers fell hissing into the melting snow amid a bursting cascade of golden sparks. Fire Chief Nate Vinal stood holding the nozzle of the hose as he watched the hell-like fury of the fire take the place of the first home he had known.

"Thank heavens, Ma got out," he said brokenly to Barnabas, as he turned the hose on the barn.

"Thank Barney," said Barnabas. "He saw the fire first."

And Nate did. The next day he rowed out to the island with Mrs. Vinal and Gramp. Gramp had learned of the fire that morning. Forgetting in his worry that a gentleman ought to shave before saying anything of an important nature to a lady, Gramp had hurried down to Hatchet Cove where Carrie Vinal was staying with Nate. Without even a nod to the rest of them as they sat eating their breakfast (indeed, he seemed to be entirely unaware of their presence), he had offered his hand in matrimony.

"I would have asked her sooner," he told Barney, who sat with Mr. Tootle in his lap and his plaster cast on a chair in front of him, "but I thought she was fonder of her boardinghouse than she was of me."

"And all the time," Mrs. Vinal admitted, "I

liked him the best of the two."

"I might never have heard her say it if it hadn't been for Barney," said Gramp gratefully.

"Thank Santa Claus," said Barney. "If it hadn't been for him, I wouldn't have had my skis. And if I hadn't had my skis, I wouldn't have had the accident. And if I hadn't had the accident, I wouldn't have been awake. And if I hadn't been awake, I wouldn't have seen the fire. So thank Santa Claus," he finished, very much out of breath.

It was quite generally conceded that silver linings did exist in dark clouds.

CHAPTER SIXTEEN

The Vultures

TWO UGLY RUMORS began to circulate through Abbidydumkeag, one about Gramp and another about Mrs. Vinal, who was soon to be called, for the sake of convenience, Mrs. Gramp. These two rumors found their roots in the great fire on the night of January fifteenth. Some of the villagers began to entertain doubts in their minds concerning Gramp and Mrs. Vinal. Those who knew them best—including the Kellyhorns—while distressed by the rumors, never for a single moment believed that there was any truth in them. There was little question as to the identity of the person who had started these stories.

A great rivalry existed between Ermina

Mink, the village gossip, and Carrie Vinal, though, to tell the truth, Carrie Vinal in the goodness of her heart never suspected it. Many years ago during the same summer that Mrs. Vinal had opened her boardinghouse Mrs. Mink had put up a sign outside her own house a few hundred yards down the road beside the general store, proclaiming to the world that she, too, took in boarders. To begin with, the two boardinghouses differed very little in size, though later Mrs. Vinal's business increased and the boardinghouse with it. The chief differences lay in their appearance. For while Mrs. Vinal's was newly painted, and freshly laundered curtains hung behind shining windows, Mrs. Mink's boardinghouse presented a slovenly aspect. The roof was a tattered and torn affair of blackened shingles, and the walls were little better. It was doubtful whether any of the boarders could see out of the windows, what with cobwebs and flyspecks. Perhaps for these reasons, or perhaps because the food when

it appeared on the table was either cold or nauseating or both, no boarder ever stayed at Mrs. Mink's for longer than three days. Sometimes, after they had checked out, Mrs. Mink would meet them the same day coming out of Mrs. Vinal's. They would look sheepishly away, pretending that they had not seen her. Each time anything of this sort happened Mrs. Mink's resentment toward Mrs. Vinal doubled in strength. At the end of the summer Mrs. Mink removed the sign from before her house. She never put it up again. In its stead appeared several years later a shiny, red gasoline pump which by now had reached the dilapidated state that all of Mrs. Mink's belongings reached. She kept herself in no better condition than she did her house or gas pump. Her dresses resembled potato sacks more than anything else as they hung from her little, bony shoulders. And her face looked as dark and evil as her house when she sat with her cronies, savoring a choice bit of gossip in the little room attached to the house where she sold greasy hamburgers and soft drinks.

The morning after the fire, Ermina Mink, while poking around the charred ruins of the boardinghouse with several other curious persons, came upon an old kerosene can which had been flung into a snowbank behind the house. Her face looked darker than ever when she returned to her house with the kerosene can in her hand. Mrs. Hawkins—a long, thin, pious woman with an acid tongue was already in the room waiting for her. But Mrs. Mink didn't explain the can in her hand. She wanted to save it until all of them had gathered. For "the girls," as the cronies called each other, or "the vultures," as old Ralph Middleby, the storekeeper, called them, met at Mrs. Mink's every morning after the marketing. There were four of them.

"Set down and make yourselves to home," said Mrs. Mink, when they had all arrived. Revenge glinted in her little eyes, revenge she had long cherished against Mrs. Vinal for putting her out of business, which, indeed, had been her own fault and no one else's. However, before she could begin, the pious Mrs. Hawkins had something to tell them that could not wait.

"My boy just come back from Hatchet Cove," she said. "He had to take some eggs up to Lem Trott's. He says—" Mrs. Hawkins dropped the words slowly and meaningfully—"he says that old fool, Sherman Drake, and Carrie Vinal have just been to the town clerk's to apply for a marriage license." After she had dropped her bomb she folded her hands and her lips returned to their usual upside-down *U* position.

"Ha," exclaimed Mrs. Mink in the silence that followed. Her eyes flashed. Carrie Vinal was going to pay double for the humiliation that Ermina Mink had suffered. "He's marrying her for her money, that's what he is," she said.

"Pfft," scoffed one of the gossips. "Carrie Vinal ain't got a cent. She put every cent she earned back into the boardinghouse."

Another vulture nodded. "And the money she put into food for them summer boarders was something, I'll tell you."

"She ain't got narthin' now," agreed Mrs. Hawkins, looking up the road to where the remains of the boardinghouse were still smoking.

"You're wrong," said Mrs. Mink. "I suppose you think she never took out a bit of insurance? I happen to know that the house and everything in it was heavily insured. Carrie Vinal's not dumb, you know. So what does she do? She finds herself without a red cent in the world. She's put everything she has back into the house. There's only one way to get the money back. And that's to have her house *accidentally* catch fire."

"But that's arson!" exclaimed Mrs. Hawkins. Even the pious Mrs. Hawkins could not believe that Carrie Vinal was capable of so dastardly an act.

"That's ex-*act*-ly what I mean," said Mrs.

Mink, producing the kerosene can. "I found this out behind her house in the snow. There wasn't a bit of snow on it so it must have been thrown there sometime *after* the snow flurry yesterday afternoon. My guess is that Carrie Vinal, when everyone was asleep, threw some kerosene up the chimney, lit it, and then tossed the can out back so that it wouldn't be found by the firemen. Then she just waited for the sparks from the chimney to light the dry shingles on the roof, hoping someone would discover the fire before she had to leave the house. Which they did," Mrs. Mink ended triumphantly.

"Yes, but she was fast asleep and the fire had almost reached her room when they found her," one of the cronies pointed out.

"Just an act," sneered Mrs. Mink. "If the kerosene can doesn't prove it to you, the fact that she and Sherman Drake are getting married on the insurance money ought to."

It wasn't hard to convince the vultures that all Ermina Mink had said was true. "If I were you," she said, as they went out the door, "I wouldn't breathe a word of this until *after* they are married. If they know anyone suspects, they won't get married. Carrie Vinal will just live with one of her children. And arson must be punished," said the wicked Mrs. Mink virtuously. She licked her chops in anticipation of the discomfiture and starvation which she hoped Mr. and Mrs. Sherman Drake would face. They could not live on the pittance that Gramp's wood-hauling business would bring in, she thought. But she didn't know that already they were discussing plans for a new boardinghouse.

So it wasn't until after the wedding a week later that the four gossips began spreading their poison and the two rumors went forth that the bride had committed arson and the groom had married her for the insurance money.

At first Gramp and Mrs. Gramp had laughed. But suddenly it grew serious. In the week preceding the wedding Mrs. Mink had not been idly waiting. By sly means she found out the name of the insurance company and for what amount the boardinghouse was covered. Having satisfactorily discovered that it was for no paltry sum, Mrs. Mink sat down at the counter and, with the help of good Mrs. Hawkins, penned a long letter to the firm in Hartford which had issued the policy, telling them among other things about the kerosene can she had happened to find in the vicinity of the fire. The result of the letter was that Mrs. Mink had a boarder for the first time in thirteen years. The insurance company had immediately sent to Abbidydumkeag an inconspicuous adjuster by the name of Smith.

For a week Mr. Smith uncomplainingly ate Mrs. Mink's bad food and looked through her fly-specked windows. He had long talks with Mrs. Mink and the pious Mrs. Hawkins. He went to the general store and sat quietly by the stove listening to old Ralph Middleby and the other men discuss the fire. He went up to

Hatchet Cove and talked to Gramp and Mrs. Gramp, who were staying at Nate's until the frost left the ground and they could start building their new home. And although he found Mrs. Mink and her food and friends distasteful and Gramp and Mrs. Gramp quite the opposite, it was his duty as an investigator to take back to Hartford the undeniable evidence of the kerosene can and a story that Mrs. Mink had made up for his benefit. Mrs. Mink told him she had overheard Carrie Vinal say to another woman that the only way she would ever get rich was to set fire to the boardinghouse. Mrs. Mink had conveniently forgotten who the other woman was so Mr. Smith could neither prove nor disprove the truth of the story before he left town.

A few days after Mr. Smith's departure, Mrs. Gramp received a letter from the Hartford insurance company saying that, under the circumstances, they would be unable to pay her anything until after further investigation.

To add insult to injury, that same morning

the unwilling sheriff of Abbidydumkeag, prodded into action by Mrs. Mink, knocked on the door of Nate Vinal's house. Mrs. Gramp opened it herself.

"Sorry, Carrie, I sure hate to do this," said the sheriff mournfully, "but I've got a warrant here for your arrest."

"That's all right, Fred," said Mrs. Gramp. She was always a good sport. "But I do hate the word 'arson.'"

"I do too," said the sheriff. "Especially when it ain't the truth."

"Thank you for thinking it isn't the truth," said Mrs. Gramp gratefully.

"I'm so durned sure of it," said the sheriff, "that I'm putting up the bail for you myself."

There were a dozen other people in Abbidydumkeag who would have been only too glad to put up the bail for Mrs. Gramp. Two of these were Penny and Pam. Even though they did not hear of the arrest until after school, when the bail had already been paid, it is doubtful whether all the coins in both their banks would have added up to the grand total which the state had asked as bond that Mrs. Gramp would appear at the courthouse in Twidboro on February 26th.

"We've got to do something," Penny told Pam. "Today is already the second and the twenty-sixth is less than a month away."

"But what?" questioned Pam. "How can you prove that a chimney accidentally caught fire? Especially when Mrs. Gramp was the only one in the house when it happened."

"Did you ever think," asked Penny, "that it might not have been an accident? That someone really might have started the fire with the kerosene in that can?"

"Penny, how can you!" exclaimed Pam. "Mrs. Gramp is one of the finest, decentest, honestest—"

Penny interrupted her before she could get any further. "I don't mean Mrs. Gramp, dummy. I mean it might have been an enemy or something."

"Mrs. Gramp doesn't have any enemies," said Pam, "except Mrs. Mink." For if Mrs. Gramp had been blind to Mrs. Mink's hatred of her, the rest of the village had not.

"I've been thinking quite a lot about this," said Penny. "I figured that if I were doing it, I would have climbed up the trellis in the back of the house to the roof. And after I had poured the kerosene down the chimney and lit it, I would have thrown the kerosene can down on the ground and slid as fast as I could down the roof to the trellis again. Then I would have run away. I'm not a criminal," said Penny, just in case Pam was beginning to have any doubts about her honesty, "but if I was one that's what I would have done."

"That's just what he did do," cried Pam, convinced that the fire had been set by an outsider. "And he forgot to pick up the can in his hurry."

"It might have been a she," said Penny, thinking of Mrs. Mink.

CHAPTER SEVENTEEN

Kidnapped

FEBRUARY HAD passed quickly. Already it was Saturday, the twenty-fourth. In two days the trial would begin, and as yet Penny and Pam had not unearthed a single clue that could prove Mrs. Gramp innocent. They had taken to dropping in at Mrs. Mink's hot dog and hamburger stand every afternoon after school in the hopes that Mrs. Mink might accidentally say something that would confirm their suspicions. But they had picked up nothing save a few pains in the stomach from bad hamburger meat.

"We've done everything we could," Penny had told Pam at breakfast that morning. "All we can do is pray that the jury will know an honest person when they see one. You might just as well catch the stage and go spend the weekend with Nancy as you planned."

"I told her that I might come and that I might not," said Pam. "Don't you think we ought to hang around the ruins just one more day to see if the criminal will return to the scene of the crime the way he's meant to in books?"

"She's meant to," corrected Penny, who was still convinced that it was Mrs. Mink who had set fire to the boardinghouse. "But I'm sure she won't," she said. Penny had given up hope a week ago.

"All right," said Pam. "I'll be back on the stage in time for supper tomorrow night."

"Pam'll get her tail feathers wet before she gets to Twidboro," Barney said, when the door slammed behind her. "I'm glad I don't have to be out in this weather." Contentedly he licked his paintbrush into a point before he stuck it in a jar of black paint.

The wind was south and a heavy fog hid everything outside the window except the misty outline of the spruce trees behind the house. This in itself would not have been unpleasant, but with the fog the sea wind brought a cold, driving rain that froze as soon as it struck the ground. Penny wandered about the house feeling lost, for this was the first time she and Pam had been separated since the day that Aunt Ivory had disappeared. In the past four months, the Twins had become as attached to one another as only twins can become. Unable to find anything on the radio but recipes and morbid continued stories, Penny finally settled down at the kitchen table with Barney.

Barney's leg was nearly well. The cast had been removed and the crutches were hardly necessary any longer. But of course he could not do anything active like skiing or skating or even going to school. The long hours at home Barney had spent in building a model of Tootle's Circus. There were little tents made of matches and old salt bags. And circus wagons painted red and yellow and blue with curlicues of tinfoil pasted on their sides. With some modeling clay from the five-and-ten in Twidboro, Barney had made little clowns and elephants and horses and tigers. He was painting these now.

"You can help with the clowns if you want," he said.

Penny picked up a paintbrush. "You know," she said a moment later, looking up from a spot on a clown's nose, "I'm beginning to think there's something in what Pam says."

At that moment Mr. Tootle (the goat, not the little clay ringleader whose top hat Barney was now painting black) came capering in from the shed. He leapt from side to side and the little bell that hung from his neck jingled. The bell had been Aunt Ivory's Christmas present to Barney.

"That bell, for instance," Penny said. "How would Aunt Ivory have ever known you had a goat to hang it on unless she knew Uncle

Conrad and Aunt Lucy?"

"Aunt Ivory never said anything about hanging it on a goat," Barney pointed out.

"Yes," said Penny, "but what else could you have hung it on? It's much too big for Tiger Boy."

"I could have hung it on my door," said Barney.

"But you don't have a door," reminded Penny.

"No, I guess I don't," Barney admitted.

"There's something very mysterious about the whole thing," Penny said, as she placed her finished clown on the table.

Sunday dawned clear and bright. It was still cold. The wind had not died down but it was from the right quarter now. And when the sun came out it made the world into a fairyland of ice. There wasn't a twig that wasn't jacketed in shining ice or a bush that wasn't dressed in spangles. In spite of the fine weather, there wasn't much to do outdoors. The skiing and the sliding had been spoiled by the thick, icy crust on the snow, and the ponds were ruined for skating. Penny would have walked to Hatchet Cove to see Gramp and Mrs. Gramp but even that was out, for they were staying at the Drakes' in Twidboro until the trial was over.

So it was an eager Penny who started off at five-thirty in the dory with Barnabas to meet the stage bringing Pam home from Twidboro. Penny walked up the crusty road to the snow-covered remains of the boardinghouse. Even though the building was no longer there, the stage through force of habit still loaded and unloaded its Abbidydumkeag passengers at the same spot it always had. Penny was alone. Barnabas had stayed behind talking to the men in Ralph Middleby's store. She reached the unloading spot just as the headlights of the stage swung around the bend in the road. The clanking of the chains stopped as Chick Gammage skidded the car to a stop on the icy road. Two people emerged from the stage.

Neither was Pam. Penny waited for her to get out. But there was no one left in the car except Chick Gammage.

"Didn't Pam come back with you?" Penny asked. It was a foolish question. She could see for herself that Pam was not there.

"No," said Chick, slamming the door. He had a good supper waiting for him at his house.

Hmm, thought Penny as the red taillight went down the road. That's funny. She said she'd be back for supper. Maybe she decided to stay up there for the trial, though. But she should have called the store and left a message. Maybe she did and Ralph forgot to tell us, Penny reassured herself.

She was just about to turn on her heel and start back for the store when a heavy hand seized her by the shoulder and the blinding glare of a flashlight fell on her face. For a minute Penny was too astonished to be afraid. But only for a minute. Then she heard the unmistakable snarl of Rusty Hanna. In the excitement of the fire and in their concern over the trial, Penny had completely forgotten that three days before the fire Rusty Hanna had been found missing from the prison. And so the information had gone in through one ear and out through the other. What did it matter now that Aunt Ivory was safe somewhere in Florida? But here he was, and evidently it was going to matter. Rusty Hanna fastened his hand more securely on the collar of Penny's coat.

"I warned you what would happen if you tried to run away," he snapped, shaking her by the scruff of the neck. "I thought I told you to stay there and mind the lines."

"I was going right back," Penny said meekly, working for time. Quietly with one hand she undid the buttons of her coat. She thought she would never get them all undone with her clumsy, mittened fingers. Before Rusty Hanna knew what was up she had slipped her arms from the sleeves and was running down the road leaving him with only the coat in his hand.

"Come back here, you little fool," he commanded, running after her. But Penny had had a head start.

He stopped following her when she reached the streetlight that stood before the store, because he could go no farther without being seen. Dropping the coat, he turned and ran in the opposite direction. Penny burst into the store.

"What's happened? Where's Pam?" Barnabas cried, when he saw her minus her coat.

"It's Rusty Hanna," Penny panted. The men by the stove had been only mildly interested when they saw her come rushing in out of the cold night with only a pair of mittens to keep her warm. But at the mention of Rusty Hanna's name they snapped to attention.

"Where is he?" they demanded, their chests expanding with the idea of catching an escaped criminal. One of them sprang to his feet and made for the door.

"I don't know," said Penny. "He chased me

as far as the store and then he ran back along the river road. I think he's kidnapped Pam and has her locked up somewhere because he told me that he had warned me what would happen if I tried to escape. I guess he thought I was Pam."

"You mean Pam wasn't on the stage?" Barnabas asked. Penny's story sounded so fantastic.

Penny shook her head.

"But where could he have taken her? Didn't he say anything else?" asked Barnabas.

"One more thing," answered Penny. "But it doesn't make sense."

"What was it?" the men demanded.

"Well, he said he thought he'd told me to stay there and mind the lines. That doesn't help," said Penny despondently.

"Of course it does!" shouted Barnabas. "He's got her locked up in a smelt house watching the fish lines."

"By gorry, you're right, Barnabas," said the men, getting up and hurrying into their coats.

"Only one place near here would be likely and that's Hatchet Cove."

"Unless it be up the river from the cove," said the man who had rushed out. He had returned with Penny's coat in his hand, but he had not seen Rusty Hanna.

"May I come, Puppa?" pleaded Penny. Barnabas said something about gunplay and little girls but the men pointed out that it might come in handy to have someone along who so closely resembled Pam. Before they hurried out into Ralph Middleby's car and someone else's, Ralph reached into a box behind the counter and brought with him two handfuls of creepers to tie on their feet so that they could walk on the ice. Without wasting any more time, they careened down the river road to Hatchet Cove.

"Even at this rate," Barnabas called over his shoulder, "we won't overtake him. He probably took the shortcut through the woods."

"We could look for his tracks," suggested one of the men.

"Won't do no good," old Ralph pointed out. "Ain't no tracks. Crust be hard enough to hold a herd of elephants." Which was true. Their search would have to start at the smelt houses on the ice near the mouth of the Alewife. When they reached Hatchet Cove they could see in the bright moonlight the row of little smelt houses stretching out toward the bay as far as the ice would hold them. For the cove here, being much more sheltered than the harbor at Abbidydumkeag, had frozen over even though the winter had been unusually mild. Smoke was coming from most of the chimneys, for it was flood tide now, the time when smelts bite best, and the houses were occupied by men fishing through the ice.

"Not likely he'd dare show his face with the others in Smelt House Row," said Barnabas.

"Won't hurt to ask," said Ralph. "Besides, we can find out if they know of any other houses off by themselves up the river."

They walked across the ice toward the smelt houses. The creepers tied to their insteps crunched as they bit into the ice with each step. Barnabas knocked on the door of the first smelt house they came to.

"What's up?" asked it owner, as the light from his lantern fell on all the men from Abbidydumkeag.

"You seen Rusty Hanna about?" asked Ralph. Thanks to his evil reputation, there was hardly a man in the county who did not know Rusty Hanna.

"Rusty Hanna!" exclaimed the man. "I reckon he's in Canada by now."

"He was seen in Abbidydumkeag less than an hour ago," Barnabas told him. "We have reason to believe that he is hiding out in a smelt house somewhere nearby. Thought you might know of one up the river. Probably in some out-of-the-way spot."

"He ain't in Smelt House Row, that's certain," said the owner of the house. "I know everyone here. Might be up river, though. Jed Simmons and Nate Vinal noticed a house up to

Roscoe's Rock a couple of weeks ago when they were out rabbit hunting. We ain't been having much luck down here, so they moved their houses up there yesterday thinking that seeing as this other fellow still had his house there the fishing might be better."

"And you don't know who it is?" asked Barnabas.

The owner of the smelt house shook his head. "They don't neither," he said. "Nate says the chimney's always smoking, but they ain't seen nobody going into it or coming out of it. I'd like to go along with you," the man said eagerly. "Haven't had but one nibble today. The rest are having the same luck. Perhaps they'd like to come too."

Ralph and Barnabas welcomed the offer. Before long, every house on Smelt House Row was dark. The army marched up the Alewife River on their creepers. They had not gone very far when they saw in the moonlight two smelt houses being dragged toward them on sleds.

When they got closer the men pulling the sleds turned out to be Jed Simmons and Nate Vinal. They were fuming and frothing about some third person whom they referred to by the names of various members of the animal kingdom. Among these could be heard dog, rat, pig, jackass, hog, rattlesnake, skunk, and so forth.

"What's up?" they asked, when they saw the army.

"What's up with you?" the army asked.

Here followed a string of names some of which had nothing to do with the animal kingdom. Nate, who was a little calmer than Jed, explained. "It's that fellow who had his house up to Roscoe's Rock," he said. "I wouldn't blame him for upping and leaving the place and going off to some place where he could have the fish all to hisself, but when we got there today the low-down critter not only had gone but he had poured kerosene through the hole he was over to drive us and the fish away." To this Nate added a string of nouns none of which Penny had ever heard before. "Only Rusty Hanna could play a trick like that," he said.

"You don't know how true those words are, boy," said Barnabas. He explained where they were going.

"He probably took his house further up the river to some little inlet where he wouldn't be followed," said Jed, as he and Nate left their houses on the sleds and joined the hunt.

"Look out for the holes," said Nate, as they passed Roscoe's Rock. Only three rectangular holes remained where the smelt houses had been.

"There's his hole, and there's the kerosene can," said Jed, vehemently kicking the can. Penny picked it up. It was the same kind of can that Mrs. Mink had found at the scene of the fire. Suddenly an idea came to her. For the first time she realized that it might have been someone other than Mrs. Mink who had set the fire.

That's just what happened, she told herself excitedly. Rusty Hanna set the boardinghouse on fire! And when I saw him he was returning to the scene of the crime just the way criminals are meant to. But why did he do it? she asked herself. She couldn't understand that. Her thoughts were interrupted by an exclamation from one of the men.

"There it is," he cried. In the light of the moon, around a bend in the river they saw a solitary smelt house close to shore. Smoke was rising from the chimney. As they approached they heard an angry voice coming from the round hole which served as a window in the back of the smelt house. It was the same voice that had curdled Penny's blood not even two hours ago.

"You might have told me there was another one," Rusty Hanna snapped. "I nearly gave myself away."

"You did give yourself away, Rusty Hanna," answered the even voice of Barnabas Kellyhorn.

Rusty's voice ceased. The light in the little house was doused.

"Here I am, Puppa! Here I am," came Pam's voice from the smelt house.

"Shut up," snarled Rusty. Unless he did something quickly, Rusty Hanna would be trapped by the horde of men bearing down upon the smelt house. He slipped out the door on the other side of the house. Skirting the river's edge in the shadows of the trees, he had passed the men before they realized what he was doing. And then he was out on the ice in the bright moonlight.

"You can't get me now!" his rasping voice shouted from behind them. "I've had my revenge. Her bones are only black cinders now!" With that sinister and cryptic remark he started running. Penny and Barnabas opened the door of the smelt house. But the others followed Rusty Hanna. Down the river they ran in the moonlight. Past Roscoe's Rock, past Jed's and Nate's smelt houses standing high on their sleds, down the river to Hatchet Cove where the little smelt houses made crisp shadows across the ice. Rusty Hanna was still ahead of them for he had creepers too as well as a head start. On they ran past Smelt House Row and past the farthest smelt house. Here the men stopped because the ice was getting thinner. But Rusty Hanna ran on. The splitting report of cracking ice whipped back and forth across the cove. Another crack and still another. And then a grating voice came back to them in the moonlight.

"You can't get me now!" Rusty Hanna cried again. Nor could they. For at that moment, amid the thunder of cracking ice, he sank into the cold, black water of Hatchet Cove.

CHAPTER EIGHTEEN

The Trial

F COURSE I don't approve of playing hooky myself," said Barnabas.

"Under the unusual circumstances it will be quite all right," said Miss Baker, excusing Penny and Pam from their classes on the morning of the 26th. They were on their way to catch the morning stage to Twidboro to attend the trial of the State *versus* Mrs. Sherman Drake.

They weren't the only ones in the stage that morning. In the front seat next to Chick Gammage sat Mrs. Mink and Mrs. Hawkins. Mrs. Mink was to testify for the state, and Mrs. Hawkins had come along to witness the discomfiture of Mrs. Mink's rival. Already their faces were triumphant. Behind them on the center seat, each with two neat, brown pigtails hanging down her back and a red plaid dress buttoned under her coat, sat Penny and Pam. Stuffed into the rear seat behind them were Barney and Barnabas and a pair of crutches. No one spoke much on the way up. They were too tense with excitement.

The courtroom was filled when they got there and the room buzzed with whispered conversations. The Kellyhorns followed Mrs. Mink and Mrs. Hawkins down the aisle between the spectators. Mrs. Gramp's children were there. And her children's children. Floyd and old Ralph Middleby were among the persons who had come up from Abbidydumkeag. Hiram Crimmins and his wife were there along with Mr. Coffin, the undertaker, and many other old friends of Pam's. And Nancy was there with her mother and father. Gramp sat beside them. His usual cheerful expression had given way to one of worry. Several reporters sat at the back of the room with bored looks on their faces. Some had cameras on their laps. Mrs. Hawkins found herself a seat near the front where she could see everything that went on. Penny and Barney took the only empty seats behind the rail that separated the spectators from the witnesses. Unfortunately these were right beside the good Mrs. Hawkins.

Pam and Barnabas continued, however, down the aisle in the wake of Mrs. Mink and took the two seats that Mr. Harrowscratch, Mrs. Gramp's lawyer, had saved for them at the table on the other side of the railing. Mrs. Gramp was already there in her purple Sunday hat. She sat talking to Nate Vinal and the warden from the prison, who sat on either side of her. She showed no signs of nervousness except for the handkerchief that she held screwed up into a ball in one hand. The only other person at the table was Mr. Harrowscratch. He was a dry, taciturn man in a pepper-and-salt suit. He never said much, but the other lawyers in the county had come to know that the words he did say could carry as much impact as a ton of dynamite. He and Barnabas immediately put their heads together and started whispering. Barnabas was explaining in detail what he had told Mr. Harrowscratch over the telephone in the middle of last night.

While he was doing this Pam looked around the courtroom. She had never found occasion to be in it before. The room was a nightmare in golden oak. Everything was golden oak, golden oak, golden oak: the paneled walls; the judge's desk and also the bookcase behind the desk filled with set upon set of legal books; the desk of the court stenographer and the witness stand; the jury box; the chairs the spectators sat in. The table before Pam was made of it as well as the table across the room where Mrs. Mink sat with the prosecuting attorney and Mr. Smith, who had come up from Hartford for the trial. Pam's eyes rested for a moment on Mrs. Mink and the attorney, who were looking with puzzled faces across the room at herself and Barnabas and the others. They had not thought that Mr. Harrowscratch would find a single witness he could call on in defense of Mrs. Gramp. Pam's heart gave a small jump in the sudden realization of the great responsibility that rested on her shoulders.

But at that moment the court clerk got up and read a long list of the names of the jurors who, one after another under the eyes of the spectators, sheepishly took their places in the jury box. No sooner had he finished than there was a shuffling of shoes and chair legs as everyone stood up for the judge, who appeared through a little door at the front of the room. If the door had been one inch narrower, it is doubtful whether Judge Nichols, even by taking a very deep breath, could have passed through and left the doorframe intact. He was a large, sloppy man, and his rusty, black gown flapped carelessly about him as he strode to his seat behind the desk. He may have had spots on his vest, but no one cared. Not even Mrs. Nichols. For his dirty vest covered one of the kindest hearts in the state of Maine and laughter wrinkles enclosed his genial mouth in a long series of parentheses. Amid another shuffling of chairs everyone sat down.

"Will the court please come to order," said Judge Nichols, rapping for silence with his gavel. The court clerk got up to inform them that the court was in session. And the trial of the State *versus* Mrs. Sherman Azariah Drake was under way to prove whether the defendant was or was not guilty of the crime of arson.

Mrs. Mink was the first person to be called to the stand. She swore to tell the whole truth and nothing but the truth, but she failed to live up to her promise. Mr. Scroggs, the prosecuting attorney, had produced the kerosene can as Exhibit A and asked her if she had ever seen it before. Mrs. Mink had said yes and told the jury how she had come across it the morning after the fire without so much as a speck of snow on it. After that she lapsed from the truth and told the false story she had made up about Mrs. Gramp. In the glow of lying she embellished what she professed to have overheard Mrs. Gramp say. And under the cross-questioning of Mr. Harrowscratch, the attorney for the defense, she again conveniently forgot to whom Mrs. Gramp had been talking and where the incident had occurred.

Mr. Smith was the next to take the stand. He corroborated what Mrs. Mink had said, but, when Mr. Harrowscratch asked him, he was only too willing to admit he had found Mrs. Gramp's reputation in Abbidydumkeag to be spotless and that all he knew of the matter was what Mrs. Mink had told him.

Mr. Scroggs had no other witnesses. Nor did he think he needed them. As far as he was concerned the fate of Mrs. Sherman Drake was sealed.

Mr. Harrowscratch was on his feet. "I move

that the indictment be dismissed," he said, "on the grounds that the prosecution has failed to establish a prima facie case."

But the charge was not going to be dismissed so easily. Mrs. Gramp took the stand in her own behalf, and Mr. Harrowscratch had only one question to ask.

"Were you fond of your boardinghouse, Mrs. Drake?" he asked quietly.

"Yes," said Mrs. Gramp. "Very fond. It had been my home ever since I was born." A tear shone in each of her eyes which Mrs. Mink, already tasting the sweet plums of victory, failed to see. But the jury was not so unobservant.

And then it was Mr. Scroggs's turn.

"Mrs. Drake," he asked, as he began his cross-examination, "where were you on the night of January the fifteenth of this year, the night your boardinghouse caught fire?" His voice was oily and he rubbed his long, pale hands together. He was going to use every means in his power to get the jury to turn in a verdict of "Guilty." "Profile" Scroggs, Gramp had nicknamed him years ago because he was so thin that you couldn't see him if he looked at you fullface. The name had stuck, much to Mr. Scroggs's resentment. Now that he had a chance to get back at Gramp he was going to use it.

"I was in my boardinghouse at Abbidydumkeag," said Mrs. Gramp.

"Was there anyone else with you at the time?"

"I was alone," said Mrs. Gramp.

"Now, tell me, Mrs. Drake, in what part of your house did the fire break out?"

"To the best of my knowledge," said Mrs. Gramp, "it started in the chimney at the south side of the house."

"To the best of your knowledge," mimicked Profile Scroggs. "Where were you at the time?"

"I was asleep," said Mrs. Gramp calmly.

"She says she was asleep," sneered Profile Scroggs, toward the jury box. "Tell me, Mrs.

Drake," he continued, turning back to the witness stand, "how many fireplaces opened into this chimney?"

"Only one," replied Mrs. Gramp. Mr. Harrowscratch had warned her about this question.

"And that was—-?"

"That was in the parlor."

"And, Mrs. Drake," snapped the prosecuting attorney, "when was the last time you used this fireplace?"

"It was on Christmas Day," said Mrs. Gramp truthfully.

"And you hadn't used the parlor since?"

"I only went in it to dust."

"Then," said Profile Scroggs menacingly, "the chimney couldn't have caught fire by itself. Or could it, Mrs. Drake?"

"No," acknowledged Mrs. Gramp, "I guess it couldn't."

"And you had everything to gain and nothing to lose if the building burned down?"

"I object, Your Honor," said Mr. Harrowscratch, jumping up. "The question is a leading one."

"Objection sustained," said Judge Nichols.

"Was your boardinghouse insured, Mrs. Drake? Against fire, for instance?" asked Profile Scroggs, rewording the question.

"Yes," replied Mrs. Gramp, twisting her handkerchief. "And everything in it?"

"Yes," said Mrs. Gramp.

"That will be all, Mrs. Drake," said Profile Scroggs, bowing theatrically.

"Are there any other witnesses?" asked Judge Nichols.

"I have four more," said Mr. Harrowscratch, standing up.

"Four!" exclaimed the bushy eyebrows of Judge Nichols. "Proceed, Mr. Harrowscratch," said his mouth.

Mr. Russell, warden of the prison, was first.

"Can you tell me, Mr. Russell," asked Mr.

Harrowscratch, "whether there was anything unusual that occurred at the prison on the night of January the twelfth of this year?"

"Yes, there was," said the warden. "A man by the name of Rufus Hanna—I believe he is known as Rusty Hanna in these parts—escaped from his cell and disappeared."

"I object," shouted Mr. Scroggs, jumping to his feet. "Your Honor, I demand that this evidence be stricken from the records as having no bearing on the case in question."

"If the prosecuting attorney will please be patient I will show Your Honor and the jury that this fact has an important and direct bearing on the case," said Mr. Harrowscratch quietly.

"Objection overruled," said Judge Nichols. "The counsel for the defense will please proceed."

"Have you seen Rufus Hanna since January twelfth?" Mr. Harrowscratch asked the warden.

"No," said Mr. Russell. "The sheriffs in

every township have been looking for him, but he hasn't turned up yet."

"One more question, Mr. Russell. Did Rufus Hanna say anything peculiar while he was in your custody?"

"Yes, he did," said Mr. Russell. "He kept making threats about a person named Ivory Perry. Said it was all her fault that he was in jail, but that he knew where she was and that he'd 'get her' before he was through."

An audible gasp ran through the Twidboro courtroom. The reporters pricked up their ears. Every one knew that Ivory Perry had disappeared, but no one suspected that there was any connection between her disappearance and the fire at Abbidydumkeag.

"That's all, Mr. Russell," said Mr. Harrowscratch.

"Has the prosecuting attorney any questions to ask the witness?" inquired Judge Nichols. But all that Profile Scroggs could do was shake his violently purple face. Barnabas's testimony came next. He told the jury about his daughter Penelope rushing into the general store after having been accosted by Rusty Hanna, about tracking Rusty down and the other men following him after his escape from the smelt house. He told how he and Penny had found Pam tied to a little chair in the smelt house with only enough of her arms free to mind the fishlines. And then Nate Vinal took the stand.

"Mr. Vinal," asked Mr. Harrowscratch, "have you ever seen this before?" He held up the kerosene can that Penny had picked up on the ice the night before.

"Ayah," said Nate, "it's the one Rusty Hanna left on the ice up to Roscoe's Rock after he had poured kerosene in the water to drive us and the smelts away."

"And you're sure it was Rusty Hanna who did this?"

"When we found him he was in the same house as the fellow who had the can," said Nate, as Mr. Harrowscratch put Exhibit B down beside Exhibit A. The two cans were identical. On both of them had been written in green paint the word "KAROSINE." No two people could have spelled kerosene that way. Mr. Scroggs's face turned from purple to pea green.

"Did Rufus Hanna say anything peculiar when you found him, Mr. Vinal?"

"Yes," replied Nate. "He shouted, 'You can't get me now. I've had my revenge. Her bones are only black cinders now!' Then he ran down the river toward Hatchet Cove. And before we could stop him, he had fallen through the ice and drowned."

"Have you anything else to say, Mr. Vinal?" asked Mr. Harrowscratch.

"Don't think so," said Nate, scratching his head. "Except that he had his rubbers on when he drowned hisself."

Pandemonium broke loose in the tense courtroom as Nate stepped down from the witness stand. Everyone had come in the fearful expectation that Gramp's bride was to be convicted of arson. Now, not only had her trial taken a turn for the better, but for the first time they learned that Rusty Hanna, whom they all had feared and hated, had met his end by drowning with his rubbers on.

"Order in the court! Order in the court!" shouted Judge Nichols.

When the crowd quieted down, Mr. Harrowscratch produced his last witness. It was Pam Kellyhorn. Her eyes were round and serious as she sat on the edge of the golden oak chair in her red plaid dress.

"Just a few questions," said Mr. Harrowscratch, "to settle the question of who set the boardinghouse on fire and why. Now, Pam, tell us when it was that you first saw Rusty Hanna."

"Last Saturday morning I was waiting for the stage in the road in front of where the fire had been. I was all by myself when I noticed someone hiding behind the chimney because that was the only thing left you could hide behind. At first I thought it was one of the kids waiting to jump out and scare me. So I decided to look. But it was a man. It was Rusty Hanna. He grabbed me and stuffed a handkerchief in my mouth so I couldn't yell and then he carried me away because he thought I would tell someone that I had seen him. And I would have, too," she added.

"Where did Rusty Hanna take you?"

"To Roscoe's Rock. He was living there in his smelt house. But when we got there, we saw two other smelt houses beside his, so we hid in the woods until the men left. It was raining, too—" here Pam sneezed. "After they left," she went on, "Rusty Hanna poured a whole can of kerosene down the hole he had been fishing through. It was just like the can Mrs. Mink found at the fire. When he wasn't looking I threw it out the window for the men who owned the other houses to find. He had tied me to a chair inside the house, and he made me sit there while he pulled the house further up the river. If he hadn't left my hands free I couldn't have thrown the can out."

"And then what?" asked Mr. Harrowscratch. "Did he tell you what he was doing at the remains of the boardinghouse?"

"Yes," said Pam. "Later, when he found the kerosene can gone, he was very angry. He said if someone found it they might discover it was just like the one that he had used when he set the boardinghouse on fire. That's what he was looking for Saturday morning. When the second can was gone he wanted to set right out to get it. I hoped that one of those men would find the can so I told him to wait until the next night because it was raining and didn't he want me to cook him some smelts. After a while he agreed. But the next night when it was beginning to get dark he went back to the place where the boardinghouse had been, because there was smoke coming out of the other two smelt houses and he didn't dare go near them. He thought that if he could get one of the cans, why then he'd be safe. That's when he met Penny, my twin. He thought she was me and that I had escaped and was going to get the can myself and then tell people where he was hiding. He was very angry when he came back, but he didn't move his house again, because he thought he was safe after all. And then Puppa and all the men came. So he ran away."

"Did he tell you why he set fire to the boardinghouse?" asked Mr. Harrowscratch.

"Yes, he did," said Pam. "He had been very angry at Aunt Ivory because she had taken his cat that his dog had bitten all up. She wouldn't give Tiger Boy back to him because he was so mean. Even when he had a gun she wouldn't. The next morning he found out that she and I—only it was really Penny—had gone down to Abbidydumkeag and that she was staying at Mrs. Gramp's boardinghouse. He got sort of crazy thinking about it in prison because if it hadn't been for the cat and Aunt Ivory he'd never have been there. So when he escaped he went to

Abbidydumkeag, thinking Aunt Ivory was still there. On the night of January the fifteenth, he climbed up the trellis in back of Mrs. Gramp's house and poured kerosene down the chimney and lit it. He was in the bushes watching all the time. The only person he saw come out of the house was Mrs. Gramp, so he was sure his plan had worked and that Aunt Ivory had burned to death in her bed." Pam was out of breath when she finished. She had never made such a long speech in her life. Not even the time she had been Antony in *Julius Caesar* in the play at school. She stepped down from the stand and went back to the table where the exuberant Mrs. Gramp nearly smothered her to death.

Mr. Harrowscratch turned to the jury, said a few words to the effect that there was nothing more to be said, and joined the happy Mrs. Gramp at the table.

Then Mr. Scroggs angrily summed up his case, pounded on the rail in front of the smiling jury, turned red, turned green, turned purple.

"I need not instruct the jury as to what verdict I feel they should hand down," said Judge Nichols, beaming, when Profile Scroggs had finished.

The jury did not even leave the room. "We have already reached a verdict, Your Honor," said the foreman of the jury without any hesitation. "The jury finds the defendant—" here he paused and continued with a broad grin— "the jury finds the defendant not guilty."

The courtroom stopped holding its breath. The crowd went wild. Cameras clicked and flashbulbs exploded. Gramp was nearly beaten to a pulp as husky hands enthusiastically pounded him on the back. And Mrs. Gramp was borne aloft by the happy, noisy citizens of Twidboro and Abbidydumkeag. Underneath the racket could be heard the sound of Judge Nichols hammering with his gavel for order in the court. But the only thing the gavel accomplished was a wide crack in the golden oak desk before him.

PART III

SPRING

CHAPTER NINETEEN

The Circus

NOW THAT THE trial was over the longing for Aunt Ivory that had never left Pam's heart (nor Barnabas's either, if the truth were known) increased tenfold. Time passed slowly. March roared in like the proverbial lion, bringing with it Town Meeting and a southeast gale accompanied by snow, hail, and rain which, though it lasted three days and drove sparrows and wood thrushes into barns, could not discourage the townspeople from attending meeting. For the rest of the month the snow along the sides of the road remained high above a person's head and the sleighs went merrily. Added to the snowy weather was extreme cold for the first time that winter. Though March continued blustery to the end, a flock of wild geese was heard honking its way up the Alewife River on the fifteenth, and before the twentieth striped squirrels and robins were seen.

In April, the ground as well as fingers and toes began to thaw, and by the middle of the month croaking frogs had taken the place of ice in the ponds. Spring came early. Fence posts were set and the cows turned into pasture. Bluets spread themselves over the meadows. And Gramp and Mrs. Gramp started breaking ground for the new boardinghouse down on Crow Point. Penny and Pam and Barney would wander down there after school, breathing the delicate spring air and wondering whether the hint in the air and the faint tinge of green on the fields was only their imagination. But it couldn't be. For though the leaves on the trees were nothing more than red and green buttons, horses were plowing and there were white violets in the woods at Crow Point. It seemed forever before the warm weather finally came. And then it did. Only a month remained of school.

Pam and Penny and Barney were walking back one late afternoon from Crow Point animatedly discussing the new boardinghouse. The main building was nearly done. In the woods behind it would be ten smaller log cabins where the boarders would sleep. The Kellyhorns had spent the afternoon picking the bunches of violets that now drooped from their warm fists, and poking around the shavings and sawdust of the new buildings. Barney's pocket bulged with bits of discarded, blue carpenter chalk that he had recovered in the debris, and Penny and Pam had pinned shaving curls before their ears. They were coming along the road in this fashion when they spied a ladder leaning against the barn where the former boardinghouse had been. A man stood on the top rung, holding in one hand a large piece of paper and in the other a wide brush such as men who put up billboard posters use.

"I hope he isn't going to ruin the looks of the barn," said Pam. From where they were they could not see what the man was pasting up.

"Look!" cried Barney, as they came closer. "It's the back end of a tiger. There's going to be a circus!"

"So there is," said Penny. For though only the right hand half of the sign was up, the word CIRCUS was written in big red letters above the back half of the tiger.

"It's going to be just like the one Uncle Conrad saw here when he was a boy!" exclaimed Pam, as the man started slapping on the bottom half of the other side with his big brush. "Look at all the roaring tigers and lions now."

"And look!" cried Barney. "There's the bottom half of a man in white riding breeches. And there's his whip."

"Oh," cried Penny, "read what it says now!" The man had finished. He gave a final slap to the poster, stuck his brush in the paste pot, and started climbing down the ladder.

"'Tootle's Circus,'" Pam read. "'Twidboro, June twentieth.'"

TOOTLE'S CIRCUS
TWIDBORO
JUNE 20

"Oh!" cried Barney. "Oh!" He jumped up and down until bits of blue chalk dropped from his pocket. "It's *exactly* like the one that made Dad run away from home."

"Not quite," said Pam. "Look." She pointed to the lion tamer. They could see every bit of the poster now that the man was no longer standing in front of the lion tamer's face. The lion tamer carried a whip, wore a pair of white pants, and was golden-haired just like the one Conrad had seen seventeen years ago. But there the similarity ended. "See," said Pam. "This lion tamer is a lady." She seemed to them the most beautiful, golden-haired lady that had ever graced a circus poster.

"I wish I was as brave as that," said Penny with awe.

"I wonder who she is?" mused Barney. "They had a man lion tamer when I was in Florida. She certainly must be brave. Almost as brave as Mummy and Dad."

"Braver," said Penny, stoutly defending her new heroine.

"Well, just as brave," said Pam, settling things once and for all.

When they got home they borrowed Barnabas's telescope. Barnabas, hungry from a day on the water, found them at suppertime still sitting on Barney's bunk as they took turns squinting at Mrs. Gramp's barn.

"Aha, a circus poster," he said, borrowing his own telescope. "There's nothing like a circus poster for dressing up a barn. "'TOOTLE'S CIRCUS,'" he read. "'Twidboro, June twentieth.' What a sly fox Conrad is! Not telling us and waiting for us to be surprised by a poster. He probably talked Mr. Tootle into coming. Why, that circus hasn't been in these parts since the time Con ran away."

"Can we go, Uncle Barnabas?" pleaded Barney.

"Of course," said Barnabas, who had never considered not going.

It seemed to the Kellyhorns that June twentieth would never come. The last month of school was endless in spite of the school play and the fun they still had fooling Miss Baker. Nothing had ever spurred on Penny or Pam toward getting good marks more than the fact that they were twins. At first Miss Baker had found herself confused by the two pigtailed girls. Soon, however, she discovered that she could tell which was which by asking one of them to solve a complicated problem filled with decimals or to spell some terrible word like *paraphernalia* or *khaki.* If the girl she spoke to was unable to find the correct figure, Miss Baker knew it was Penny. Or if she couldn't spell, she knew it was Pam. But by the time spring came this system began to fail. Spelling correctly became second nature with Pam, and to Penny decimal points and interest rates were old friends. When the final exams in Spelling and Arithmetic were handed in, both Penny's and Pam's papers said "P. Kellyhorn" on the outside. If the twins had expected to find Miss Baker wearing a puzzled expression on the day she handed back the papers, they were disappointed. She did not hesitate about whom to hand them to. For both Penny and Pam found written under their names in big red numbers "94%" in Spelling and "95%" in Arithmetic.

Finally, however, the day of the circus arrived. The twins and Barney were all for getting up at dawn and going up to Twidboro to see the circus put up. But Barnabas advised them to wait for the stage, which would get them there in time for the parade. So after breakfast they rowed across the harbor to catch the stage, leaving Mr. Tootle at home chewing on a tuft of pink clovers. But, of all days, the stage at the last minute came down with some mysterious ailment. There was nothing left to do but wait while Chick Gammage lay on his back underneath the car trying to diagnose the trouble. It was noon before he had found what was wrong. And they had missed the parade. Barnabas was talking to Floyd down on the wharf while Chick monkeyed with his sick car. Penny and

Pam and Barney, with long faces, sat in a clump of daisies watching Chick. It was late afternoon when he finally emerged from beneath the stage.

"She's as smart as she ever was," he told the trio. His face, covered with black grease, beamed triumphantly. So it wasn't till suppertime that they reached Twidboro. The Drakes had invited them for an early supper so that they would be in plenty of time to see the sideshow before the performance in the big tent started. Gramp and Mrs. Gramp had been invited too.

After supper they all started down Elm Street to the same field where Tootle's Circus had raised its tents seventeen years ago. It looked exactly the way Penny and Pam and Barney had imagined it would except that the tents looked grayer and dingier. But once inside the gates this was forgotten in the raucous calls of "Popcorn!" and "Peanuts! Feed the elephants! Get ya peanuts here!" The warm smell of popcorn and peanuts and hot dogs engulfed them. Pinwheels were madly spinning at one booth. Another sold fur monkeys dangling on sticks, and birds whose tails whistled when you waved them in the air. "Wheee," screamed a bird, as the attendant switched the stick the bird hung on above the heads of Penny and Pam. At another booth were cowboy hats and whips, and Kewpies dressed in red and blue feathers. There were as many adults present as boys and girls. The smallest children were lost in the depths of the crowd, but here and there a balloon floated up from the hand of some unseen child, and now and again a small boy came racing through the forest of legs, switching a whip before him. The Kellyhorns and the Drakes pushed their way into the sideshow tent. But there were just as many people here as outside, and all they could see were the heads of the performers: the bored faces of the Fat Lady, who wore a pink ribbon in her hair, the Living Skeleton, and the Blue Man. Then they saw the sword swallower in the act of thrusting a long, curved sabre down his throat.

"Boy! It's Dad!" cried Barney, who could see better than any of them from his high perch on Barnabas's shoulder. "I thought he had given up swallowing swords."

"If only we could get near him," said Pam. For they stood at the back of the crowd. But even by pushing very rudely and roughly they didn't reach him before a loudspeaker announced that the show in the big tent was about to start. The sideshow performers disappeared. And the crowd shoved its way through the exit.

The circus was everything they had expected. There were women in spangles and men in tights and elephants and ponies and glitter and lights. The band never stopped playing except when Mr. Tootle, who was the ringleader, came out in his top hat to announce that the greatest or the most breathtaking or the most death-defying act in the world was about to thrill the audience. He announced Lucy and Conrad Kellyhorn's flying act with all three of these superlatives. And they lived up to them. The crowd gulped and gasped and Barney held his breath until it was over. Then he swelled with pride. In between this and other acts there came the clowns—clowns wearing shoes three feet long, clowns on stilts, and clowns who kicked each other in the seat of the pants while the crowd split its sides with laughter. But there was one clown that they noticed more than all the others. It was nearly the end of the show when he appeared. This one did not jump around hitting or being hit by the other clowns, but went seriously about his business in the center ring. He had five white cats with him that he made lie down in a row and then roll over. He snapped his fingers and they all stood on their hind legs and began to walk around the ring.

"Why, those are Aunt Ivory's cats!" exclaimed the twins and Nancy in one breath.

"There's James and David. I'm sure of it," said Pam. "And there's Daniel."

"Do you think she sold them to the circus?" asked Penny.

"Maybe she needed the money," said Pam. Suddenly the glitter of the circus seemed tawdry and remote as Pam thought of Aunt Ivory. Even the winter on Indian Island seemed nothing more than a dream and she realized that the happy times there had not erased the misery she had felt in being separated from Aunt Ivory.

"Pam," came Barnabas's voice from far away. "Look!"

Pam turned her eyes. Barnabas was pointing at the clown with the cats. Though his face was hidden beneath white paint and red spots, though his baggy trousers were so stuffed with padding that he was unrecognizable, there was something familiar about the way he was walking.

"We don't have to hunt any further," Barnabas told Pam quietly. "That's Aunt Ivory there."

Pam watched the clown lean down and gently stroke the head of one of the performing cats.

"Yes," she said, hardly daring to breathe, "I do believe it is."

CHAPTER TWENTY

The Queen of Cats

PAM AND BARNABAS stood up as the shrill whistle in Mr. Tootle's mouth told the clowns to cease their antics. After a hurried conference they had whispered to each other that it would be best not to rouse the hopes of the others lest their suspicions about the clown proved wrong. They were about to start for the dressing rooms when Penny looked up from burying her face in a young pillow of pink candy floss.

"Where are you going?" she asked. "It's not over yet. The lion-tamer lady hasn't come in yet and the popcorn man said she was last. They're putting up her cage now."

In the center ring the men were erecting the

steel arena for the grand finale while in the two end rings girls hung by their jaws high in the air, swirling colored scarves with their arms. Mr. Tootle had announced them as the "Iron Jaw Butterfly Girls." Barnabas and Pam hesitated despite their eagerness. Then because it was apparent that the show was almost over, they sat down again. No sooner had they done so than there was a long blast on Mr. Tootle's whistle. The Butterfly Girls dropped fluttering to the ground as every light in the tent went out except four bright spotlights that fell on the cage in the center.

"You are about to witness the most breathtaking, most stupendous, most astounding, and the most amazing and most dangerous act that it has ever been the privilege of this circus to present to the public," cried Mr. Tootle. At the word "dangerous" the men standing outside the cage laid their hands on the holsters of the revolvers at their hips. "I now present to you that daring young lady who defies death itself as she puts her troupe of savage jungle cats through their paces." Mr. Tootle bowed. "Here she is! Miss Ivory Perry!" At these words Aunt Ivory ran gracefully into the spotlight, her arms embracing the audience. She wore white riding pants, and in her hand she held a whip. The spotlights made her hair shine like gold. Then she turned and entered the steel arena, closing the gate behind her.

"All right," she called to the man who held the sliding door that let the lions and the tigers into the wire tunnel that led to the cage. The man raised the door. Pam held her hands over her face though she watched all the time through her fingers. The others were so astounded at seeing Aunt Ivory that they sat with their mouths open. They, as well as all the people from Twidboro, had gasped when she was announced.

"Ivory Perry!" everyone had exclaimed. They were caught unaware by her sudden return, a return as sudden and bewildering as her disappearance nearly eight months ago. After a few seconds they began to recover from their initial surprise. But they were more bewildered than ever. Here was Ivory Perry, the disappointed maiden lady who had lived quietly at Number 11 Elm Street with five cats and a niece, patching quilts, here she was in breeches—white ones too—and shiny boots making tigers and lions climb up steps to sit in pyramid formation. No, it could not be she, they kept saying. This Ivory Perry with the fluffy, golden hair was not the one from Twidboro. Yet they knew she was. Never had they watched a circus act with more interest, not even when they saw Conrad Kellyhorn from Abbidydumkeag fly somersaulting from one trapeze to another at the top of the tent. Nor did Barnabas's eyes leave the steel arena one instant. His fists were tightly clenched, and his mouth was a thin line of suspense.

"What a fool thing to do," he muttered to himself. "She can't possibly have had enough experience." He clenched his lips tighter and nervously reached for a cigarette in his pocket. He held it unlit in his mouth, watching. Though she controlled the big cats only with her whip and her eyes, Ivory Perry seemed to have no difficulty except with one thundering lion who wove back and forth on the ground for a while and refused to climb to his perch. Finally, however, the last great tiger had leapt lightly onto the lowest perch and the pyramid was complete. Except for the paw of the belligerent lion which kept darting out toward Aunt Ivory and the roars he now and then emitted, the jungle cats might have been made of yellow marble. Ivory Perry stretched forth her arms and bowed to the breathless audience. Barnabas breathed a sigh of relief and lit his cigarette. That was when Aunt Ivory lost her control over the angry lion. All during her act her eyes had never once left the big cats. But now, bowing in the direction of Barnabas, she saw his face in the light of his match. For a moment she forgot the cats. The thunderous lion seized his chance. He sprang from his high perch down upon Aunt Ivory.

"Oh, my God!" cried Barnabas. He was out of his seat before he had said it and racing down the aisle. The tent was filled with the screams of women and the cries of children. Once Barnabas had to sidestep a woman who had fainted into the aisle. And then he was out in the center of the tent.

"Give me that gun, you idiot," he cried. Without waiting for permission he seized a revolver from one of the stupefied guards outside the cage. Barnabas was inside the cage now. A shot rang out over the crowd as he fired the gun at the lion. The lion, terrified by the shot, though there was no harm done since the gun contained only blank cartridges, raised his head and roared. Again Barnabas fired, and this time the lion began cautiously to back away, leaving Aunt Ivory on the ground. By now the guards had come out of their stupor and were vigorously firing their blank cartridges at the already subdued lion, forcing him into the wire tunnel. Barnabas Kellyhorn had Ivory Perry in his arms. Mr. Tootle opened the gate for them as he carried her out.

"How is she?" he asked, his voice croaking with worry.

"She's alive," said Barnabas, "but her arm is bleeding pretty bad." She lay white and unconscious in his arms. "We'd better get a doctor."

Mr. Tootle found his microphone. "Is there a doctor in the house?" came an enormous voice through the loudspeaker. Perhaps it was this or more likely it was something that Barnabas said quietly into her ear. At any rate, Ivory Perry opened her eyes. And, when she saw where she was, her cheeks grew pink again and she smiled gloriously into Barnabas's eyes. The crowd, seeing that she was not only alive but happy, went wild with relief. As they disappeared in the direction of the dressing rooms, six rousing cheers filled the tent, three for Ivory Perry and three for Barnabas Kellyhorn. The twins and Barney found them later in the trailer that served Aunt Ivory both as home and dressing room. Dr. Cox, who had come to see Conrad perform, had just finished sewing up the wound in Aunt Ivory's arm.

"Keep the dressing wet," he said as he was leaving, "and I'll be back to see you tomorrow."

"Tomorrow!" exclaimed Aunt Ivory. "Why, we're leaving at dawn tomorrow." She winked at Dr. Cox.

"You don't seriously think you're in any condition to leave tomorrow," said Dr. Cox, winking back. "After the shock you've had and with that arm, you had better stay at Number 11 Elm Street for a while. Doctor's orders, Ivory."

"Well—" said Aunt Ivory. And then she saw Pam standing in the doorway. "All right," she said as Pam rushed into her one good arm.

"Oh, Aunt Ivory," Pam sobbed, drowning Aunt Ivory's bosom in all the tears she had saved up for eight months. "Why did you leave me for so long?"

"Pam," said Barnabas (for once there was no doubt as to whether it was Pam or Penny). "Pam," he said, "I don't think Ivory feels well enough for explanations."

"Of course I do, Barnabas," said Aunt Ivory, gathering the rather large Pam into her somewhat small lap. At that moment Conrad and Lucy came in and a lot more hugging and kissing took place before Aunt Ivory told her story. Pam had shifted her seat to the more sturdy lap of Conrad Kellyhorn, Barnabas had Penny on his knee, and Barney was being held by his mother. Then it was that Aunt Ivory explained her sudden departure and her equally sudden return.

"It was just as I said in the note," she said. "When I saw you and Penny together, Pam, I knew that you two belonged with each other and with Barnabas and that you no longer needed me."

"But I did!" Pam interrupted. "And I do."

"Let me continue, Pam. That's what I thought at the time. And then I saw what Gramp and Mrs. Vinal . . ."

"Mrs. Gramp now," said Barney.

"Lord," said Conrad, "I forgot. The Drakes are all waiting outside to see how you are."

"Call them in," cried Aunt Ivory. Before she went on there was more hugging and kissing and this time congratulations.

"Anyhow," she continued, "when I saw what everyone was trying to do, I decided to run away."

"Just as I said," said Mrs. Gramp.

"I knew that you all wanted to be together. And I am sure you children sincerely wanted me to come to Indian Island as Barnabas's wife."

The Drakes and the Kellyhorns, with the exception of Barnabas, looked at each other in amazement that Ivory Perry should talk so boldly.

"However," Aunt Ivory went on, "I believed that Barnabas did not really want this himself and that if he appeared to enjoy my company it was only for the sake of you children. If I had gone back to Twidboro to live, Pam perhaps would have followed me."

"I did," said Pam, "but you weren't there."

"If anyone knew where I had gone, I might have been followed."

"I nearly went to Palmetto Beach," said Barnabas, "but Conrad and Lucy assured me that you weren't there."

"When I was young," Aunt Ivory continued, "there were two things I wished to do. The one I wished the most never happened. But the other wish was to join the circus. Of course, a respectable, proper girl like I was, whose father was a minister, didn't do things like that. Nor could I with a clear conscience have left my mother and father alone after the first wish had not come true. Just before they died Kitty had the twins. I took Pam because it was all that Barnabas could do to manage one baby. And my life continued along in the same rut. So when the time came for me to turn Pam over to her father, I decided to disappear and join a circus. I had the cats, so I thought perhaps I might get a job. And I did. In Palmetto Beach with Mr. Tootle. He needed a clown with a performing troupe of animals. It took a lot of convincing, but finally he said I might go along with them. In the meantime, I was to understudy Madame Zuba who was the lion tamer. Mr. Tootle has been hard up this year. That's why we've all had to double up on our acts. Conrad had to be a sword swallower as well as a trapeze artist. I met him and Lucy almost as soon as I got there. I realized at once that Conrad was the younger brother whom Barnabas used to speak of so fondly. Though he thought he was considered something of a black sheep in Abbidydumkeag, he didn't know that everyone loved him even more than before for being such a colorful one. It didn't take long for Conrad to discover who I was either. He used to talk to me about Abbidydurnkeag and Barney and how both he and Lucy would like to go back there to live.

But he kept talking about how he was a black sheep and how if he were not taken back into the fold Barney might be the one to suffer. I finally persuaded him to go back. And I wrote to old Ralph Middleby, for I had heard he was going to retire as soon as he could find someone to buy his store. In return Conrad promised not to mention to anyone that I was in Palmetto Beach."

"He certainly fell over backward doing it, too," said Barnabas.

"You see, Barnabas had kept writing letters to Palmetto Beach asking me to come back and marry him. And I kept thinking it was all for Pam's sake so I never answered them. I knew if I stayed away long enough she would get over it."

"But I didn't," said Pam.

"You would have," said Aunt Ivory. "So I intended to spend the rest of my life with the circus. But a circus isn't the glittery, happy, noisy thing the audience thinks it is. It's hard work and sweat and dirt and long hours. Perhaps I wouldn't have minded any of these if Barnabas hadn't written such sweet letters telling me about Pam and Penny and Barney and the snow and the island and all the other good Maine things I love. It made me very homesick. I slightly altered my plans. I decided to stay just one year. By then Pam would have forgotten me."

"No, I wouldn't," Pam cried. "Oh, Aunt Ivory!"

"I wouldn't have come near here. I didn't know what towns we would play. Tootle's Circus hadn't been here for seventeen years, so I didn't think it would be again. Then the night before the tour started Mr. Tootle said Twidboro was on his list. It was too late to back out. Anyhow, I was a clown. And nobody in town, even when they saw the five white cats, would have suspected that under all the grease paint and pantaloons was Ivory Perry. Ivory Perry, the minister's daughter!" Aunt

Ivory laughed. "I guess I would have fooled them all right. But two nights ago, Sam (that's the lion that bit me) had one of those mean spells and we had to leave Madame Zuba back at the hospital in Kittery. I made an awful fuss with Mr. Tootle about going on today. He said, all right, he'd let me on this afternoon, but that I had to go on tonight because we couldn't disappoint the crowd. The posters were up everywhere of the yellow-haired Madame Zuba taming the lions. So I went on. And here I am. That's the end."

"Not quite the end," Barnabas reminded her.

"No," Aunt Ivory smiled, "not quite." She blushed. "Barnabas and I are going to be married," she said. "I'm sure he loves me now. He wouldn't have risked his own life for mine unless he did."

"If the doctor is making you stay in Twidboro," said Barnabas, "perhaps we can have the wedding before you leave to finish the tour."

"Perhaps I was teasing," said Aunt Ivory. "Perhaps I shan't be leaving at all." In this case, "perhaps" meant "of course." "Besides, I have a quilt to make before next fall."

And there was a June wedding, after all. Conrad Kellyhorn had not persuaded Mr. Tootle to reroute the circus tour for nothing.